At the landing to the basement, the door opened and a security guard stepped into the stairwell. He glanced at the two foreigners and his hand went to his sidearm.

He barked an order in Russian, flipping open his holster.

Weiss held up his hands and spoke in English. "No trouble here. No trouble. Just visiting Dr. Malenkov."

Vaughn, standing next to him with the cooler of tissue samples in his hand, stopped and waited.

At the mention of Malenkov's name, the guard looked up and down the stairs. He could see that Malenkov wasn't with them, and his expression hardened.

He shouted something at them. Weiss felt a chill run through him. Up until now, things had gone smoothly. But now they were trapped in a stairwell with a nervous guard, who spoke no English.

As time stretched and Dr. Malenkov did not appear, the guard grew more agitated. Vaughn watched the guard's hand as his fingers flexed around the grip of the Stechkin APS. With twenty rounds, he didn't even need to be a good shot.

ALIAS™

THE **apo**™ SERIES

A TOUCH OF DEATH

BY CHRISTINA F. YORK

An original novel based on the
hit TV series created by J. J. Abrams

SSE

SIMON SPOTLIGHT ENTERTAINMENT
New York   London   Toronto   Sydney

S|S|E

SIMON SPOTLIGHT ENTERTAINMENT

An imprint of Simon & Schuster

1230 Avenue of the Americas, New York, New York 10020

Text and cover art copyright © 2006 by Touchstone Television.

All rights reserved, including the right of reproduction in whole or in part in any form.

SIMON SPOTLIGHT ENTERTAINMENT and related logo are trademarks of Simon & Schuster, Inc.

Manufactured in the United States of America

First Edition 10 9 8 7 6 5 4 3 2 1

Library of Congress Control Number 2006925831

ISBN-13: 978-1-4169-2446-3

ISBN-10: 1-4169-2446-9

CHAPTER 1

NAGATAKA CHEMICAL RESEARCH FACILITY
OSAKA, JAPAN

In the hushed laboratory, fluorescent light reflected off the stainless steel surfaces. Although it was dark outside, inside the sealed building modern technology maintained an optimum working environment around the clock.

Two scientists in spotless white lab coats stood at a workbench covered with beakers and test tubes. Occasionally one would pause to write his observations in a notebook on the desk behind him. They were lost in their work, oblivious to the guard at the end of the hall and the faint noises of the nightly cleaning crew as they went about their duties.

That is, until five men with guns burst through the door of the lab.

The intruders were dressed in military fatigues, with black balaclavas obscuring their features. Without speaking, two pairs of men grabbed the startled scientists, frog-marching them across the laboratory to an unused workstation. The scientists were shoved facedown on the floor, their hands lashed behind their backs.

Two of the intruders then moved back toward the leader. The other two upended their rifles and cracked the butts against the skulls of the prostrate scientists before joining the rest of their team.

Moving swiftly and silently, the five men swept through the laboratory. They ignored the racks of test tubes, the rows of beakers, and the cupboards of rare chemicals. Instead they moved deliberately toward a single work station deep within the laboratory.

The leader's eyes glinted with anticipation through the cutouts of the dark mask of his head covering. He opened a refrigerated cabinet under the counter and pulled out a wire basket, holding four tightly capped vials of sapphire-blue liquid.

The rest of the team formed an arc around him, facing the rest of the room. There would be no surprises while their leader accomplished his mission.

Removing his gloves, he picked up one of the vials with extreme care and held it up to the light for a moment, as though admiring the jewel-like color, then nodded his satisfaction before returning the vial to its place.

From within his jacket, the leader withdrew a small metal box. He worked the latches and the top opened, releasing a ribbon of smoke that slid over the edge of the box and trailed toward the floor. His motions were deliberate as he removed each vial from the basket and placed it into a corresponding hollow within the metal box, securing each of them with a fitted cover.

When the vials were secured, he closed and locked the box and put it back inside his jacket.

Turning back to the door, he stepped through the arc of armed men and signaled them to follow him. They were gone as quickly and silently as they had come, leaving the two scientists where they had fallen, crimson blood slowly seeping from their wounds and soaking into the starched whiteness of their lab coats.

APO HEADQUARTERS
LOS ANGELES, CALIFORNIA

Arvin Sloane tapped the keyboard on his desk, shutting down the flat-screen monitor. He swiveled his chair around and faced Jack Bristow. Sloane's graying brush cut, deeply lined face, and dark, hooded eyes made him appear brooding and solemn.

It was a look that fit the enigmatic head of the CIA's black ops division, APO. It was also a look that hid much of Sloane himself, shielding his true nature and intentions from the people around him.

Jack, perhaps the person who knew Sloane better than anyone else, waited for Sloane to speak. A lifetime of service in covert agencies had given Jack the discipline to wait forever if he needed to. Though patience may not have been his natural inclination, it was a trait acquired so long ago that it had become an integral part of him.

Sloane sighed, resting his chin against his fists. He tented his index fingers and tapped the tips against his lips, a familiar stalling tactic.

When Jack still did not speak, Sloane glanced up at him and leaned back in his chair. "Those vials were the only thing taken. They represent the preliminary results of a top secret antiviral research program, a program in which the CIA has an interest. Nothing else was touched. These people knew what they were after, and the mission was clearly rehearsed. Did you recognize anyone?"

Jack shook his head. "No one." Now he could see the uneasiness in Sloane's eyes, a hint that some unpleasant surprise was contained in the images from Osaka.

"I suppose," Jack continued, "that I might recognize one of them if their faces weren't covered. But under the circumstances . . ." He let his voice trail off, putting Sloane back on the spot.

Sloane shook his head, as though trying to dispel his worries, but the uneasiness lingered in his expression. "I thought . . ." He paused, looking away, then returned his gaze to Jack. "The two scientists are recovering, and nothing was disturbed except those vials. The intruders made no effort to disguise what they were doing, as though they didn't care whether they were seen.

"But there was something about the leader. He reminded me of someone I know—*knew*. An Alliance officer in the Far East."

Sloane stood and paced behind his desk.

"Which is ridiculous, of course. All the ranking Alliance officers were killed or captured in the raids."

Jack raised an eyebrow.

"Except me." He nodded his acknowledgment. "But I had help, and a lot of information the CIA wanted. Even then, I would have been executed had you not intervened. No, it couldn't be an Alliance officer."

Jack watched Sloane as he dismissed his fears, but it was clear Sloane hadn't entirely convinced himself. There was a lingering shadow of doubt, a shadow Jack Bristow knew would have to be dispelled.

"Who did you think it was?"

"A North Korean officer named Gai Dong Jing." Sloane waved a hand, as though dismissing the thought, then thought better of it. He sat down and turned back to the monitor. With a few swift keystrokes, he restarted the surveillance video, showing the lightning raid on the research facility in Osaka.

The two men watched as the five intruders entered the lab. There was no wasted motion, and none of them spoke. Each of them knew his part in the raid and performed it without hesitation. They were not distracted by the presence of the scientists, nor tempted by rare and costly chemical stores.

As the leader removed his glove, he revealed a dark spot in the webbing between the thumb and forefinger of his right hand.

Jack leaned forward and pointed at the screen. "What is that?"

Sloane stopped the video and tapped the keyboard, zooming in on the image. As it came into focus, the screen showed a mass of dark lines and circles tattooed on the hand.

The angle was awkward, and Sloane advanced the video through a few frames until the man on the screen raised the vial to the light, giving them a better view of the hand.

The tattoo was an elaborate design, but neither man could identify it.

After a moment, Sloane spoke. "It doesn't mean anything to me," he said, shaking his head. "We should get the image to Marshall—let him run it, and see what he can find."

It didn't take long for Marshall Flinkman, APO's resident technical wizard, to come up with an answer—an answer that created more questions than it resolved.

"It isn't a single tattoo," Marshall said, laying a series of glossy photos across the sleek surface of the conference room table, the last one facedown. "As you can see," he said, pointing to the first picture, "the pattern at first appears to be quite intricate: lots of lines and angles and circles, a random design, not structured. But as you look closer"—he motioned to the second photo—"you can see variations in some of the lines. When I ran a spectroscopic analysis of the color gradients, definite layers emerged."

He gestured to the next photo. "Parts of the tattoo had faded. The differences were subtle, not really visible with the human eye, because, well, you know the human eye can only register color and light within a certain restricted spectrum, right?" Marshall didn't wait for an answer, but rushed ahead, carried by his enthusiasm for his subject.

"These differences were so small I had to devise a special algorithm to separate out the variances, and run about a thousand iterations, to make sure the results were accurate, and create the separations, and, well . . ." Marshall paused, took a deep breath, and turned over the last photo.

Sloane and Jack stared at the photo. The stricken look on Sloane's face spoke volumes.

Under the layers of obscuring tattoos was a single, simple image: the Eye of Rambaldi.

Apparently, the Alliance wasn't nearly as dead as Sloane thought it was.

The silence was like a fourth person in the room, a presence that could be felt, if not seen. Arvin Sloane affected a posture of nonchalance, leaning back in his chair and looking at the photo, as though acting unruffled would mean the situation was less critical than it actually was.

Jack Bristow wasn't fooled. Sloane was badly shaken by what he had seen. Jack turned to Sloane and stared, his eyes hard. It was time for Sloane to speak up.

"Is it Jing?"

"I don't know, Jack." He shrugged. "The tattoo means nothing. It could be anyone—a low-level Alliance officer who escaped, a field operative in deep cover, or even a Rambaldi fanatic who wasn't involved with the Alliance at all."

Oblivious to the tension between the two old friends, Marshall pulled another stack of papers from his folder and laid them on the table. "I figured you'd want to know who it was, and since I couldn't trace the tattoo—not that I'm not trying, because I am, I just haven't had any luck yet—I took the liberty of analyzing the man's face . . . well, as much as I could, what with most of it being covered."

Marshall shuffled through the papers and handed Sloane and Jack each a stack of copies. "His eyes were the only really visible part, so I concentrated on them, measured the distance between the pupils, the alignment of the eyelid fold, elevation from the bridge of the nose—you know, the usual sort of things."

"Yes, Marshall." Jack's tone was brusque, impatient. "What's the point of all this?"

"Well, the man is definitely Asian. Acting on the obvious assumption—that he was a member of the Alliance—I ran the biometric data against all known Alliance officers of Asian extraction. The check produced a list of possible identities, ranked by probability; that's the second page there."

Sloane and Jack turned to the second page. The list of names was short, with Gai Dong Jing in the second position.

"And?" Sloane demanded.

"And"—Marshall's exuberance deflated, like a day-old party balloon—"according to all the files, each of these men was either captured or killed in the raids. None of them could be our man."

Sloane nodded. "Just to be sure, Jack, I want you to run a complete check on everyone arrested or killed in the raids. Our *allies* are not always as vigilant as they should be. Call me as soon as you have any results. And don't mention any of this to the rest of the team, not until we have something to give them."

Sloane stood, dismissing Marshall, who gathered his files and retreated to his laboratory, leaving Sloane and Jack alone in the conference room.

"I'll reach out to my contacts and see if there's been any word about Jing recently. If he is alive, which I doubt, he's bound to have left a trail somewhere besides here," Sloane said, pointing to the photos.

Jack nodded. There was nothing more to say. He gathered his copies of Marshall's work and left.

When Jack approached Sloane's office two hours later, Sloane waved him in, signaling that he was on the phone. Jack sank silently into the chair across the desk from Sloane, and waited for him to finish his conversation.

Punching the disconnect button, Sloane removed his telephone earpiece and dropped it on the desk, then looked expectantly at Jack, whose usual grim expression held no clue to what he had found.

"It's as we feared," Jack said. "I checked every record from the raids, the bodies that were identified, and the follow-up interrogations of those who were incarcerated. There is no mention of Gai Dong Jing in any of them. I finally found his name on a list from the Hong Kong raid, listing him as 'missing, presumed dead.' But there is no record of his body being found. Our Mr. Jing may not be as dead as we presumed him to be."

"If it is him," Sloane said, "he appears to have access to good information and a well-trained and equipped team."

Jack nodded. "Have you been able to find anything more?"

Sloane shook his head. "Not yet. My contacts are understandably circumspect about sharing information, but I have opened some lines of inquiry that I hope will prove fruitful. A raid such as the one in Osaka requires advance preparation—recruitment, training, intelligence gathering. The trail is there. If we can find it and follow it, it'll lead us to all our answers."

Sloane rose and walked around the desk, taking a chair next to Jack. "He had to have planned for this, Jack. He must have felt there was a chance the Alliance would be destroyed, and he had a fallback position in case of just such an eventuality. He held back something from the Alliance, hiding his assets, hoarding them. We will have to find that something in order to stop him."

Sloane leaned forward in his chair and stared hard at Jack. "You wonder how I know that? How I can tell what the man must have been thinking?"

Sloane waited, the question hanging in the air. He really didn't expect Jack to answer him.

Holding Jack's gaze, his quiet voice carrying a note of almost fanatical conviction, he answered his own question. "I know, Jack, because it was precisely what I did."

CHAPTER 2

CENTRAL POLICE STATION
VLADIVOSTOK, SIBERIA

As the station clock moved toward midnight, Nickolai Kerinski waited impatiently for his shift to end. It had been a quiet night, with too much of what passed for coffee on the evening watch burning his throat, and he was anxious to get home.

Only forty minutes until his relief arrived, and then he could head home for a delayed supper. His wife had promised to wait to eat with him and he could imagine the rich aroma of the stew she was preparing, the sweet luxury of honey on her homemade biscuits. His stomach rumbled in anticipation.

The reception area was empty, the scarred benches and chipped counter smudged and worn in the harsh fluorescent light. Behind Kerinski's counter, a warren of offices and interrogation rooms was mostly dark, with an occasional pool of light from an isolated desk lamp marking the late-night location of a detective or officer with no place better to be.

The buzzer to the outside entrance sounded, alerting Kerinski to a visitor. As he turned his attention to the front door, he was surprised to see a man in a shiny silver hazmat suit, complete with hood, shoe covers, and gloves, enter the station.

The man looked and sounded like he could have come from another planet. The respirator on his suit hissed with each breath, and he moved awkwardly toward the desk.

Kerinski could see the man's face through the plastic shield in the front of the hood, though it was slightly distorted. With a policeman's practiced eye, Kerinski sized up the visitor: tall, gaunt, his face thin and drawn, eyes dark against the pallor of his skin.

His shuffling gait was due to more than the clumsiness of the bulky suit; he seemed unsteady, as though worn down by a long illness.

Kerinski tensed as the man approached him, his hand sliding beneath the counter, toward the button that would summon backup. He wasn't a timid man—you didn't last in a city like Vladivostok if you were—but the situation was steeped in danger. The suit could conceal a myriad of weapons, or the man could be preparing to unleash some unspeakable biological terror.

Kerinski hesitated, his finger on the button. The memory of the sarin attacks in the Tokyo subway was vivid. If this was an attack, he would only be calling more officers to their deaths.

But he had to warn them.

The man was at the desk now, holding his gloved hands up near his face, palms out, a posture of appeasement and surrender.

"Help me."

Kerinski held his finger in place. "What kind of help do you need?"

"My name is Peotr Alexyeev, and I have done many terrible things. I want to surrender."

The name meant nothing to Kerinski. He had not heard it in his daily briefings, nor had it appeared on a fugitive alert. Whatever terrible things this man had done, they had not come to the attention of the Vladivostok authorities.

Taking his finger off the signal button, Kerinski plucked a form off a stack on his left and picked up a pen with his other hand. He entered Alexyeev's name at the top of the form and began asking questions.

"Spell your last name, please."

Alexyeev complied, his voice strained and distorted by the suit's respirator.

"Address?"

"I do not have a local address. I have been staying with"—he hesitated—"an *associate*."

"And who is looking for you, Mr. Alexyeev? To whom do you wish to surrender?"

"No one is looking for me. They do not know what I have done. But I am prepared to pay for my crimes. I must."

"Your crimes?" Kerinski dropped his hand back below the countertop and edged his fingers nearer the button again. If he called someone in, they could deal with this crazy man and he could go home to dinner.

"Yes. I have been responsible for many deaths. Many deaths." Alexyeev choked, struggling with the words. "Strangers, yes, but my own children, also. And my dear wife. All dead. All my fault."

A chill ran down Kerinski's spine, and he pressed the alarm button. The man might be crazy, but there was something in his voice—strain and anguish that ran deep.

Crazy or not, Alexyeev believed he had caused the deaths of many people, including his wife and children. And a man who believed that, whose soul carried that guilt, had little to lose.

"You are confessing to murder?" Kerinski asked. "You say you killed your family?"

"They are dead. It is my fault. I must accept my punishment." Alexyeev stiffened and placed his hands flat on the counter, the silver suit rustling with his movements. "But there is something I must do first. There is a greater evil, and it must be stopped."

Behind him, Kerinski heard the heavy tread of booted feet approaching the reception area, then a confused shuffle of footsteps and barely muffled exclamations. He glanced over his shoulder just long enough to catch sight of the open stares of the three other officers on duty.

Turning back to Alexyeev, he tried to resume his interview.

"Evil?" It wasn't a word Kerinski was used to hearing, at least not in the police station. Here they dealt with facts, the laws, and those who broke them, not abstract concepts.

"Evil." Alexyeev repeated the word with conviction. For him, there was no abstraction. "He is evil, and we must stop him."

"Who—?" The question died on Kerinski's lips. His answer was coming through the front entry, wearing military fatigues and accompanied by four armed men. He wasn't a superstitious man, and years of police work had destroyed any belief in coincidence. He knew instantly that this was the man. The automatic weapon slung over his shoulder, exactly like the ones carried by the four men behind him, only reinforced what Kerinski already knew.

The leader moved swiftly to the counter, grabbing Alexyeev by the arm. "Peotr, you have work to do," he said in Korean. "Time to go."

The Korean was six inches shorter than the gaunt Russian, but he was clearly in better physical condition, and he began pulling Alexyeev toward the door. His team stood in a half circle behind him, their weapons held loosely, pointed toward the counter where Kerinski stood, frozen.

Despite being physically outmatched, Alexyeev struggled to free himself from the grasp of the Korean.

"No. Let me go!" he shouted.

Alexyeev thrashed his arms and legs in an attempt to throw off his Korean captor.

Struggling with the awkward mass of the man in the suit, the leader was unable to secure his weapon, and it clattered to the floor.

Still screaming, Alexyeev dived for the weapon. He got one gloved hand on it, but the leader grabbed it at the same time. The two men tumbled to the floor, wrestling over the weapon, which waved wildly around the room.

The Korean troops turned to watch the struggle, looking for an opening to intervene, taking their eyes off Kerinski.

Without hesitation, Kerinski dove over the counter, a short, stout riot club in his hand.

Alexyeev was *his* prisoner!

Behind Kerinski, the other officers moved forward, drawing their weapons and crouching behind desks and file cabinets, searching for whatever cover they could find.

Kerinski raised the club, swinging it down on

the head of one of the Koreans. The Korean staggered, and the man next to him swung around to confront Kerinski.

The second man rammed the butt of his rifle into Kerinski's stomach, doubling him over and sending him to his knees. He slammed the butt against Kerinski's nose, then reversed the rifle, swinging the barrel toward him.

A hail of gunfire erupted from behind him. Instinctively, Kerinski flattened himself against the floor as the bullets sailed over his head.

The Korean's rifle clattered on the worn tile as spots of blood blossomed across his chest. He crumpled to the floor, his face slack.

The two remaining Koreans whirled to face their assailants, unleashing a barrage of automatic gunfire.

Paralyzed by pain, Kerinski didn't move. He heard more gunfire, distant and fuzzy. Blood from his shattered nose ran into his mouth, thick and salty, choking him.

One eye was swollen shut, and the other refused to focus. Dimly, he could see shapes, three dark and one silver, moving toward the door.

The shapes disappeared, but the deafening

noise of the brief gun battle left Kerinski unable to hear the buzzer or the sound of the outside door closing.

For one tantalizing instant as blackness closed in on him, he could smell his wife's stew.

LOS ANGELES ZOO
LOS ANGELES, CALIFORNIA

Sydney Bristow accepted the ice cream cone Michael Vaughn held out to her as they stepped away from the service window at the snack bar. The sun was warm on her bare arms, and the soft swirl of vanilla was already drooping, a single drop sliding down the side of the cone.

Syd grinned, causing dimples to appear in her cheeks. She stuck out her tongue and caught the errant drop before it ran down onto her hand. Vaughn, smiling back, performed a similar maneuver.

They strolled across the walkway, pausing to look back along the path they had taken to climb the hill. The crowd was thin on this weekday after-noon, a few young mothers with toddlers or strollers, and the occasional retiree.

Sydney and Vaughn were enjoying a rare afternoon off together. Syd had eagerly accepted

Vaughn's invitation to spend the day at the zoo. Still unsure of their relationship but determined to rebuild it slowly, a normal date—an afternoon without mission briefings or impending disasters— seemed like the perfect way to enjoy their day off.

So far, that had been true. They had walked for what seemed like miles through the low hills that dotted the zoo, wandering from one exhibit to the next. They had visited the Children's Zoo, watched prairie dogs pop out of their tunnels, and spent a quiet half hour in the darkened koala exhibit.

The reptile house, a series of interlocking hexagons, was one of Syd's favorites. Although she wasn't fond of snakes, they were compelling to watch.

Now, warm from their latest uphill stretch, Michael had bought ice cream cones, and they had found a spot of shade as a refuge from the sun.

Across the path was the top of the giraffe enclosure. Down the path, back the way they had come, was the enclosure itself, with the back wall rising to meet the uphill portion of the path.

An adult giraffe, nearly twenty feet tall, pushed his head against the fence and snaked his long, black tongue between the bars, reaching for the tender green shoots of a plant alongside the path.

"Now, he," Vaughn said, gesturing to the giraffe, "would have no trouble with ice cream."

"And I do?" Syd asked, the laughter in her voice taking the challenge from her words.

Vaughn watched her for a moment, his eyes soft with affection.

She was a striking woman. Tall and slender, she carried herself with the grace of a dancer or a martial artist. Her little-girl braids made her look younger and softer than she was, though Vaughn knew better. She was a trained and deadly agent, smart and capable.

But for right now she was just Syd.

"You seem to be doing okay," Vaughn said as she took another lick of her ice cream. "Still . . ." He gestured at the giraffe, whose prehensile tongue was systematically stripping the leaves from the plant and pulling them into his mouth.

Syd watched the giraffe for a moment, captivated by his eyelashes. They were longer than any other animal's she had ever seen, and she savored the peace of the moment. Standing there with Vaughn, eating ice cream, and watching a giraffe eat leaves—it was like being a regular person.

But APO agents were not regular people, and peaceful moments came rarely, if at all. Sydney's cell phone rang, its insistent tone interrupting her temporarily calm life.

She flipped the phone open and answered it.

On the other end of the line, her father's voice dragged her out of her normal afternoon, and back into the job that consumed her life. "We need you at headquarters. How soon can you get here?"

Before she could answer, she heard Vaughn's phone beep, and she knew without asking that he was getting a similar call. Somewhere a crisis was brewing, and they were needed.

"Give me twenty minutes," she told Jack, and hung up. There was nothing more to say.

Beside her, Vaughn disconnected his call and dropped his phone back into his pocket.

The two agents exchanged a look, then started down the hill toward the parking lot. On the way, Sydney dropped her half-eaten ice cream cone in a trash can, and Vaughn did the same.

What did normal mean, anyway?

CHAPTER 3

APO HEADQUARTERS
LOS ANGELES, CALIFORNIA

Sydney and Vaughn left the commuter rail car at the end of the line. They loitered in the station until they were alone, then walked a few yards down the track. There, in a niche in the tunnel, was a service door, with a battered metal sign that read AUTHORIZED PERSONNEL ONLY.

Vaughn pulled an unmarked key card from his pocket and swiped it through the grubby card reader on the wall next to the door. The door took a moment to unlock, and then Sydney swung it open and stepped through, with Michael behind her.

Inside, the room looked like a regular electric junction room, just like dozens of others scattered throughout the city's subway system. Sydney swiftly went through the maneuvers that activated a hidden door.

She always got a little rush when she accessed the secret entrance to APO headquarters. Even after all her years as an agent, there was something exciting about opening the secret tunnel, pausing for a security scan, then continuing on into the black ops division.

They had come directly from the zoo without changing clothes. Their casual attire, which would attract no attention at the zoo or on the train, seemed at odds with the sleek glass and high-tech interior of the office.

Sydney and Vaughn headed for the conference room, where she could see her father, Arvin Sloane, and Marshall Flinkman waiting. The rest of the team was filtering into the room: Sydney's recently discovered sister, Nadia Santos; her partner, Marcus Dixon; and quiet, dependable Eric Weiss.

Syd slid into a seat at the table, forcing herself to relax. Even though CIA Director Hayden Chase had placed Sloane in charge of APO, Sydney didn't trust him. He had given her plenty of reasons to doubt him over the years, and she wouldn't easily forget his betrayal.

When he had recruited her into SD-6, the international cartel for which he had worked, she had been young and idealistic. She had believed she was working for the "good guys," and discovering the extent of Sloane's lies had nearly destroyed her. SD-6—and Sloane, specifically—had cost her the life of her fiancé, Danny, taken away her closest friends, and deepened the divide between her and her father.

She was slowly repairing the damage Sloane had caused, rebuilding her relationship with her father, learning to love again. She had discovered a sister she hadn't known she had and become close friends with many of the people she worked with. She was surrounded by people who cared for her, but there was always the presence of Sloane, a constant reminder of all that had happened to her over the years.

The muted conversations halted as Sloane passed a copy of the mission briefing to each of the assembled agents. Sydney glanced at the stack of reports, then turned her attention back to Sloane's stern face as he stood up and passed his gaze over the group assembled around the table.

"What we have here," Sloane said as he stood near the bank of video screens that covered one wall of the conference room, "is a ghost, a man who is supposed to be dead, a man the CIA thought had been eliminated with the rest of the Alliance."

Sloane nodded to Marshall, who tapped a few keys, bringing the video screens to life.

Sloane stepped back and watched, his arms folded across his chest, as Marshall took over. "This is a feed from one of the surveillance cameras in the Central Police Station in Vladivostok. That's on the southern tip of Siberia, near the Sea of Japan. It's a busy shipping port and has one of the highest crime rates in Russia. It's supposed to be a favorite place for the Russian mafia, which, by the way, shouldn't really be called the mafia, because 'mafia' is actually a Sicilian word—"

Marshall stopped suddenly, placing a fingertip against his lips, and focused his attention back on the screen. "Anyway, this video shows a raid on the police station."

Marshall ran a video clip featuring a tall man in what looked like baggy tinfoil coveralls. The man approached the reception counter and spoke to the officer in Russian.

"If you look on page three of the mission briefing," Marshall said, "there's a transcript of the audio. We had to work a little to make it all out—there were some problems with the feed we picked up. I think there was a battery too close to the audio pickup, and it was creating a hum . . . but never mind. We cleaned up as much as we could and translated it. Although"—he looked around the table—"you're all fluent in Russian, aren't you?"

Marshall paused for a second, then continued. "But there's some Korean, too, in just a few seconds here."

The team watched and listened, referring to the transcript for verification, as the scene played out.

The man in the silver coveralls had a breathing device of some kind in his suit, and his words were hard to distinguish. Even with her excellent Russian language skills, Sydney was grateful for the fast work of the engineers and translators.

The man identified himself as Peotr Alexyeev, a name that did not mean anything to anyone at the table.

When he claimed to be responsible for multiple deaths, including those of his family, Weiss leaned forward, puzzled. "Why are we interested in murders in Russia? We have plenty of those here."

"It's not the murders," Jack murmured. "It's the murderer, and his companions."

Weiss bit his lip, feeling the rebuke, even though Jack had maintained a neutral tone and had not raised his voice. Even without inflection, Jack managed to squelch any further questions.

The video continued, and they watched as the team of fatigue-clad men entered the police station and tried to drag the first man away.

It was over in a matter of a minute or two. By the end of the clip, four policemen and one of the raiders lay in pools of their own blood, and the man in the strange suit had been pulled out the door by the remaining attackers.

Marshall froze the video on the image of the four fallen officers as the last of the attackers moved out of the frame.

Sloane stepped in front of the screens. "We believe this man"—he gestured to the back of the last attacker, barely visible in the door frame—"is Gai Dong Jing, a dead man."

Sloane waited, looking around the table at a ring of blank faces, except for Marshall's and Jack's. He seemed to savor the drama of the moment, to draw power from the rising tension, as the rest of the team waited for his explanation.

"Mr. Jing was an officer of the Alliance. According to the initial report from the Far East, he was killed in a raid on a cell in North Korea. But, like Mr. Twain, the reports of his death appear to be greatly exaggerated."

Sloane turned to Jack, nodding to him to continue the briefing. "As Mr. Sloane said, it appears that Jing was not killed in the raid on Alliance posts in the Far East. We don't know how he evaded capture or why he was not listed among the missing, but we have analyzed these pictures, along with an earlier report, and we are convinced Jing is still alive."

Sydney's heart was racing, the roaring in her ears blocking out the rest of what her father said. She had worked so hard to destroy the Alliance! She had sacrificed so much, in the name of ridding the world of their evil.

And yet, here it was, the monster that refused to die. After nearly four years, it rose in front of her.

She glanced to the left of her father, where Arvin Sloane stood immobile, watching the scene play out. Anger burned in Sydney, acid tearing at her stomach as she looked at Sloane, a walking, breathing symbol of all that she had come to despise.

If he had survived, why couldn't she believe that others had as well?

Below the table, Sydney clasped her hands in her lap, fingernails digging into her palms, as she struggled to bring her anger back under control.

Her heart slowed its galloping pace, and she concentrated on breathing slowly, drawing air deep into her lungs. Her personal feelings didn't matter—not here, not in this room. What mattered was Jing, who he was, why he was a threat, and how they would neutralize him.

The time for anger would be later, after the mission was completed, after this last remnant of the Alliance was obliterated, the threat eliminated.

Sloane cleared his throat, and all eyes turned to him. "Word has reached me," he said, "that Jing may be trying to rebuild his Alliance cell."

Sydney bit back an angry remark, and Sloane continued. "We know who his contacts were, and most of them are accounted for. What we don't know, and what we need to know immediately, is who his current allies are—who is working for him or with him?"

Sloane placed his hands on the table and leaned forward.

"Jing is looking for what he calls 'partners.' He claims to have a valuable asset, one that he is willing to share for 'the right price,' and he says he needs money to produce a powerful bioweapon. But he has revealed nothing beyond that. We know he has approached many of his old North Korean associates and assembled at least a small cell, as the video clearly shows. We also know that he led the same group on a raid two days ago. A top secret biochemical research facility in Osaka was infiltrated, and an experimental compound was taken. Nothing else. They were in and out in a matter of minutes.

"These raids were fast and efficient. He knows what he wants, and he doesn't waste time on anything else. It is up to us to figure out exactly what it is he's after and stop him."

At a signal from Sloane, Marshall backed up the video a few frames, and Sloane glanced at the frozen image behind him as he continued. "It certainly does not appear that Mr. Alexyeev is cooperating with Jing, but looks can be deceiving. On the other hand, an AK-47 can be very persuasive."

Sloane looked around the table. "I want Dixon, Sydney, and Nadia in Vladivostok immediately. Find out everything you can about the police station raid. There is one survivor, the officer at the reception desk, Nickolai Kerinski. Sydney, you need to talk to him, find out what he knows. Dixon, I want you and Nadia to masquerade as South Americans with money to invest. Wheels up in three hours, and I want a full report on your plans before you leave."

The three agents nodded. Dixon closed his briefing file and rose to his feet. "If you'll excuse me, I'll get to work immediately. But I do have one question before I go."

Sloane cocked his head expectantly and gestured for Dixon to continue.

"What is Alexyeev wearing?"

Marshall tapped a few keys, zooming in on the tall figure in silver. As the video image of Alexyeev grew on the screen, Dixon's eyes widened in recognition. He said exactly what the rest of the team was thinking.

"He's wearing a hazmat suit."

Sloane smiled, as though a prize pupil had scored well on an exam. "Yes, he is. The real question is, why?"

CHAPTER 4

SEA OF JAPAN
OFF THE COAST OF VLADIVOSTOK, SIBERIA

The night sky hung low and black over the lumbering form of the battered freighter *Hinyu* as it left the harbor at Vladivostok, one ship among the many that called at the busy port.

As the *Hinyu* reached the Sea of Japan and turned east, the horizon ahead of her lightened with the coming of the dawn. The sun did not pierce the heavy, cold clouds, but faded the sky from black to gray.

Below deck, three beefy men in hazmat suits made their way along a corridor. One carried an

AK-47, its barrel tipped casually toward the floor. In front of him, the other two dragged a fourth man between them.

The captive was tall and thin. His bare chest was sunken, his arms scrawny. He had open sores across his back. The tattered remains of an old-fashioned undershirt hung from his narrow shoulders, exposing the dark bruises that covered his chest and arms. Faded drawstring pants flapped around his legs as he stumbled down the corridor on bare feet. Goose bumps covered his body, a silent protest against the chill of the lower decks. One eye was swollen closed, and his nose looked like it had been broken.

It was Peotr Alexyeev.

When they reached a hatch, one of the men released Alexyeev long enough to open the door. They shoved him ahead of them into the sick bay. In contrast to the oppressive atmosphere outside the compartment, it was brightly lit, with modern medical equipment fitted into custom-built cabinets.

In the middle of the room, bolted to the floor, were two state-of-the-art hospital beds. Their chrome rails were lowered, and nylon restraints hung from the sides.

The men dragged the prisoner to the nearest bed and lifted him onto it. While the armed man held his weapon at the ready, the other two strapped Alexyeev to the bed. They were fast and efficient, but not gentle. Alexyeev cried out in pain when the strap was tightened over his chest, pushing the open sores on his back against the stiff sheet beneath him and compressing his bruised ribs.

When they were satisfied the restraints were properly tightened, they covered his body with layers of rough wool blankets, disguising the worst of his injuries. His face was exposed, as was his left hand, which rested on the chrome rail, his wrist secured to the side of the bed, the lead clipped to his finger.

As they worked, the ship wallowed through the swells, rolling the bound man from side to side, pushing him against the restraints. He moaned, a low sound of pure pain.

"Silence!" the leader of his guards snapped in Korean. "Be grateful Colonel Jing still considers you of value. Otherwise we'd have put you in the cold water of the ocean, instead of a warm bed."

Alexyeev tried to protest, but one of his guards immediately shoved the tube of a respirator into his open mouth and held it in place while the other guard taped it securely to Alexyeev's face. With his mouth covered, he was forced to breathe slowly and carefully through his damaged nose.

Fear showed in his one good eye as he realized the fragility of his air supply. Any problem, any interference, and his body would lose the precious oxygen it needed to continue functioning.

"Not to worry," the lead guard said, but his harsh tone did nothing to allay the scientist's fears. "There will be someone watching you at all times." He nodded toward a surveillance camera attached to a bulkhead. "Colonel Jing says you are very valuable. He always protects his assets."

While the leader spoke, the other two attached electrical leads to Alexyeev; one monitored his heartbeat, and a clip on his finger kept track of his blood pressure. The strap across him registered the rise and fall of his chest as he breathed.

The wires ran from Alexyeev's bed to a cart full of electronic equipment. Lines moved across a screen in sync with the steady beeping of the heart monitor. At regular intervals a computer snapped to life, storing the current readings, and the unblinking eye of the surveillance camera watched over it all.

The leader took a moment to silently inspect the work of the two guards and nodded his approval. Without further comment, the three men walked out, leaving Alexyeev alone in the infirmary.

He wasn't alone for long.

Within a few minutes, Colonel Jing entered the room, accompanied by an attractive young woman. Her dark hair and slight build indicated her Korean ancestry, but her cornflower blue eyes contrasted sharply with her olive skin and were the mark of European blood.

Jing wore a hazmat suit, similar to the one Alexyeev had worn when he was kidnapped. The woman, in contrast, had on a sharply cut business suit of soft gray wool, the skirt hanging discreetly just above her knees. Perhaps in deference to the motion of the ship, she wore black canvas deck shoes instead of high heels.

Jing's face was covered by the hood of his suit, and the respirator distorted his voice as he spoke to the woman.

"Please accept my apologies for this, Ms. Kono." He gestured at the suit. "I am working in the lab, but I wanted you to meet our newest colleague, Peotr Alexyeev."

The woman smiled briefly at Jing, a nervous movement of her mouth that had little to do with happiness. "You are a busy man, Colonel. It was good of you to take the time to introduce me personally."

"Not at all." Jing's expression was obscured by the hood, and with his voice distorted, she could not tell whether his sentiment was genuine.

"Unfortunately," Jing continued, "Dr. Alexyeev is somewhat indisposed at the moment." Jing led the woman nearer the bed. "As you can see, he has sustained some injuries—an automobile accident, I'm told, on the way to the dock this evening." Jing glanced at the clock on the wall. "I suppose I should say last night, but I have been working all night, so it doesn't seem that it's nearly morning."

Kono flashed her nervous smile again and turned her attention to Alexyeev. He was bruised and battered, and he couldn't speak because there was a respirator tube in his mouth held in place with surgical tape.

"Will he be all right?" she asked.

"His injuries have been attended to," Jing replied. "And we have a doctor waiting in Tokyo to administer whatever other treatment is necessary."

Kono reached out, her slender fingers grazing

the back of Alexyeev's hand. His eye widened, and he tried to pull his hand back, but the restraints prevented any movement.

"You will be working with Dr. Alexyeev when we reach Tokyo. The ship's doctor says he should rest for a few days, but he should be able to resume his research in a week or so."

The ship rolled with the action of the wind and waves, and Jing took a small step to compensate. Kono stumbled slightly, tightening her grip on Alexyeev's hand to steady herself.

Alexyeev thrashed against his restraints.

Kono instantly released Alexyeev's hand, her hand flying instinctively to cover her mouth. "I am so sorry," she said to Alexyeev. "Did I hurt you?"

Alexyeev shook his head but couldn't speak, though he struggled to. The exertion formed beads of sweat on his brow that trickled down his forehead and threatened to run into his eyes.

Jing walked to a supply cabinet bolted to the bulkhead and fumbled the latch open. His gloves were ill suited to delicate movements, but Kono didn't seem to notice the discrepancy between his attire and his supposed lab activities.

Reaching into the cabinet, Jing withdrew a

stack of soft towels and carried them over to Alexyeev's bed. He set the stack on the end of the bed and handed the top one to Kono, gesturing toward the sweat on Alexyeev's face. "There is cool water in the dispenser," he said, motioning to a tank on the side of the utility cart, fitted with a spigot.

Jing turned back to close the cabinet, leaving Kono to dampen one corner of the towel and press it to Alexyeev's perspiring brow. He shrank back from her touch, but she persisted, talking in a low voice as she wiped his face.

"You must be feverish, Dr. Alexyeev. I hope this will make you a bit more comfortable." As Alexyeev grew more agitated, she became calmer, as though his helplessness relieved the pressure she felt.

Jing managed to close the latch on the supply cabinet and returned to Alexyeev's bedside. The scientist's good eye darted back and forth between Jing and Kono, and his body practically quivered with the effort to move.

After a moment, Jing spoke. "I apologize again for the circumstances, Ms. Kono. Dr. Alexyeev is hardly himself. I suspect it may have something to do with the medication he received following his accident."

Jing placed one gloved hand under Kono's elbow and gently pulled her away from the bed. "Perhaps this wasn't the best time for you two to meet after all. I hope you will not think poorly of him, or me, for this."

Jing had moved Kono toward the hatch as he talked, and now he opened it, urging her into the corridor. "I'm sure he will relax if we just let him rest. We can continue our conversation later, once I have finished my work in the laboratory."

She was in the corridor now, with Jing pushing the hatch closed from inside the infirmary. "I will come see you as soon as I am through," he promised, "and we can discuss our plans for Tokyo."

Jing secured the hatch and remained by the door, listening to the fading footsteps as Kono walked away, then moved back over to the bed where Alexyeev lay.

Jing reached down and yanked the tape off of Alexyeev's mouth, loosening the respirator tube. The tube fell away and Alexyeev sucked in a deep breath, his lungs expanding painfully against the deep bruises on his chest.

"She's a lovely woman, don't you think?" Jing said. Even with the distortion of the respirator, his voice was filled with menace, his tone cold and hard. "Compassionate. Caring. A sweet woman." He spat the last word: "Weak!"

Alexyeev strained to see Jing's face with his one good eye, anguish contorting his features. "Why? Why did you do that?"

Jing walked around Alexyeev's bed, forcing him to twist his neck as he tried to follow Jing's movements. Jing pulled back the blankets from Alexyeev, running his eyes over the damage to his body and nodding.

"Why?" Alexyeev repeated.

"Because," Jing replied, "you need to understand what we are doing here, Dr. Alexyeev. There is much more at stake here than Ms. Kono's life— or yours. You must realize that your life is not your own anymore, Doctor."

"You didn't need to kill her, Jing. There was no reason she had to die."

"I didn't kill her, Doctor. You did. You *will*. Her weakness and yours will kill her. And you will have to live with that."

Alexyeev closed his eye, trying to shut out the truth of Jing's words. He had caused other deaths, from a distance, but he had been able to explain them away, to excuse and dismiss them—until he was unable to excuse the deaths of his daughters and his son. Those were his fault, and he had been forced to watch them sicken and die.

And his wife.

He told himself it wasn't his fault, that he had done nothing, but he knew it wasn't true. If he had told her, if she had known the truth, she might have survived. He could have saved her if he had been strong enough to confess his part in the childrens' deaths.

Now Kono would die, because he had been unable to face the truth, until it was too late—until Jing had found him and made him part of his plan, until he had become someone he didn't want to be.

Now, Alexyeev knew, the only way he could fight Jing was from the inside. His only recourse was to remain where he was and wait for the opportunity to sabotage Jing's research.

It was all he had left.

Jing pulled the blankets back over Alexyeev. "There will be a lot to do when we reach Tokyo, Doctor. Get some rest. I need you to be ready to go to work."

Jing walked out of the room, leaving Alexyeev alone with the beeping of the monitors, the unwavering eye of the surveillance camera, and his own black thoughts.

"I killed her," he whispered. "My lies killed her."

CHAPTER 5

FLOWERING LOTUS BAR
VLADIVOSTOK, SIBERIA

Dixon placed his hand under Nadia's elbow, guiding her through the dim interior of the Flowering Lotus. Nadia's hair hung loose around her bare shoulders, the flowing curls framing the delicate, exotic beauty of her face.

Expensive-looking earrings dangled from her ears. Multiple strands of diamonds wound around both wrists, and a single perfect ruby hung from a gold chain, the gem nestled in her cleavage, emphasizing the curves displayed by the strapless red cocktail dress that hugged her body.

Every man in the bar, and a couple of the women, watched her progress as she swayed through the crowd on her towering heels. Beside her, Dixon was as close to invisible as he would ever be.

The hum of conversation dwindled to a whisper in her wake, then rose again when she reached the far side of the room.

The agents took a table in a far corner, Nadia draping her fur stole carelessly across an empty chair. She sat on one side of the table, Dixon on the other, both of them angled to keep their backs to the wall. It wasn't an accident that no one could approach without being seen, and anyone who joined them would have to sit with their back to the room.

"We're in place, Phoenix," Dixon murmured into his comm.

"Roger that, Outrigger." From her position in a van outside the bar, Sydney Bristow acknowledged Dixon's message and linked his conversation to headquarters, where Vaughn and her father were monitoring the operation. "Any sign of Vladimir?"

"Not yet," Dixon answered. "But your sister made sure everybody knows we're here." There was a chuckle in his voice. "Or at least they know *she's* here. I don't think anyone even saw me. I guess it's about time to change that."

With a careless flick of his wrist, Dixon tossed a money clip stuffed with American greenbacks onto the table. The hum of conversation that had resumed in Nadia's wake rose sharply. Voices were pitched higher, signaling the increased interest in the newcomers.

"I think we have their attention now." Dixon spoke quietly into the comm again. "Vladimir should know very soon that we are here, if he doesn't already."

"Let me know when he arrives," Sydney answered. She glanced at the monitors in front of her, showing the street outside the van and the entrance to the Flowering Lotus.

There was little traffic—a few luxury sedans, and the occasional tourist taxi dropping passengers at the large hotel on the opposite side of the street.

The Flowering Lotus was clearly a popular nightspot. Each time the local bus stopped, a chattering group of well-dressed young men and women would alight and crowd into the club.

Judging by the noise spilling out of the club

into the street, the DJ had started the night's entertainment. Sydney could hear the steady thump of a
hip-hop bass line and the rapid chatter of a rap
lyric in Russian.

Another bus stopped, and a cluster of young-
sters moved toward the entrance to the Flowering
Lotus. From a side street, two people too mis-
matched to be considered a couple joined the group
as it reached the front door. They disappeared in the
crowd as they passed through the entrance, but not
before Sydney caught sight of them.

"Outrigger," she said softly, "I think you'll have
company in just a moment." She glanced down at
the surveillance photo the local operative had provided after his meeting with Vladimir. "Looks like
Vladimir has a woman with him."

"Phoenix, this is Evergreen." Nadia's accent was
deliberately thick, in keeping with her cover story. "I
see him now, and there is a woman with him."

Sydney listened carefully, adjusting a control
on her audio panel in an attempt to filter out the
background noise. She managed to improve the
signal slightly and got a muttered "That's better"
from her father at the Los Angeles end of the
uplink.

She grinned at the relieved undertone of her father's comment. Two years ago, she wouldn't have understood his reaction. Six months ago, she would have understood and been angry that he hadn't been there to be annoyed by the loud music she'd played as a teenager. But now she was learning to accept her rebuilt relationship with Jack and to value their new status.

It was a beginning.

From their vantage point in the corner, Nadia and Dixon watched the odd couple make their way across the club. The man looked like exactly what he claimed to be: a longshoreman from the busy port at Vladivostok. His hair was too long to be fashionable, and his creased and stained work clothes were out of place in the trendy club. He glanced around as he walked past the dance floor, his posture clearly stating that he would be much more comfortable in a dimly lit waterfront dive where the only music came from a tinny jukebox.

The woman could be considered well-dressed, if she were going to a business dinner. But her conservatively cut dark gray suit, sensible pumps, and silk shirt with a stock tie were as out of place as her companion's workman's garb among the miniskirts, short shorts, and tank tops in every color known to modern chemistry.

They rated a few quizzical glances, but the crowd mostly ignored them, shrugging off their curiosity and continuing to dance.

The duo approached Dixon and Nadia's table, and Dixon stood to greet them. His movements were fluid, with no wasted energy, but combined with his height, the effect was imposing. His custom-tailored business suit did little to disguise the power in his body, and everything to advertise the money he expended on his wardrobe.

His dark face and deep brown eyes were impassive, and he maintained a carefully neutral expression. Still, he gave the impression of strength, agility, and ruthlessness, all barely contained.

He greeted the new arrivals in Russian, then quickly switched to heavily-accented English. "You must be Vladimir. Viktor"—he gave the name of the local CIA informant—"described you exactly."

Dixon waved toward the empty chairs at the table. "Please, have a seat. We have a lot to talk about."

A waiter materialized at Dixon's side, drawn by the irresistible pull of large-denomination American currency the way a shark is drawn to blood.

Dixon switched back to Russian and rattled off an order for two bottles of expensive champagne. As the waiter withdrew, his eyes shining in anticipation of the commission he had just earned on the overpriced wine, Dixon laughed loudly. "Nothing but the best for our new friends, right?"

Nadia glared at him with disapproval. "This is your idea of being inconspicuous?" she sneered, her words rapid and her South American accent thick. "This is being discreet? Don't you think our old friends at home might hear about what we're doing?"

Dixon's face hardened, and he lowered his voice to a tight growl. "Let's treat our new friends good, *mi querido*. And we'll talk about this later."

Vladimir had watched their exchange with undisguised glee, but the woman with him had averted her cornflower-blue eyes and turned her face toward the dance floor to watch the mass of gyrating bodies in front of her.

Dixon paused for a moment. After a lengthy silence, he nodded at her, and his voice returned to its silky softness. "Forgive me, *mi corazon*. Of course you're right. We should be careful."

Turning to his guests, he resumed as though nothing had happened. "Vladimir, you haven't introduced us to your companion."

Dixon leaned toward the woman, drawing her attention from the dance floor with his words. "I am Señor Javier Bautista, and this is my wife, Ximena Fernandez. And you are?"

The woman turned and met Dixon's gaze. "Kai. You may call me Kai. Do not pay any attention to this one." She waved at Vladimir. "He is a petty thug, with little brains and no manners."

Dixon nodded but said nothing, waiting for Vladimir and Kai to make their offer. He had let it be known that he and Nadia were in Vladivostok looking for investment opportunities, and they were not particular about the source of the profits, as long as they were large.

Dixon was acutely aware that they were in a city where organized crime was rampant. They had made sure their cover story did nothing to threaten the local power. Rather, they were looking for investments outside the local operations.

Their approach had been tailored to tempt Jing, and it appeared to have worked.

Vladimir bristled at Kai's remark. "You can't talk about me like that."

"I certainly can," Kai replied.

But she didn't look as confident as she tried to sound. Beads of sweat formed at her temples and ran down her face, trapping strands of her dark hair. Her eyes were cloudy, and her olive skin was flushed.

The waiter materialized at Dixon's elbow, carrying two bottles of wine and a quartet of champagne flutes. Dixon pulled a pair of large bills from the clip on the table and handed them to the waiter. "That's all for now," he said, dismissal clear in his voice.

The bills disappeared into the waiter's pocket, and Dixon guessed that they would never see the inside of the cash drawer.

Dixon busied himself pouring the champagne and handed a glass to each of the women. Nadia took a long sip from the crystal flute, her lips leaving a faint ruby stain on the rim.

Kai accepted her glass, but immediately set it on the table. Dixon could see a slight tremor in her right hand that jostled the bubbles in the pale gold of the wine.

"You can go," Kai said to Vladimir. It was clear she did not want to talk in front of him.

Dixon nodded to Vladimir and offered him one of the bottles. "Maybe you can find someone to share this with?" He looked pointedly at the crowd on the dance floor.

Vladimir shot him a sullen look but accepted the bottle and walked a short distance away. He kept glancing back, but Nadia shooed him off.

When Vladimir had moved off, Kai finally began to talk.

"He really is nothing more than a hired thug," she said. "He doesn't actually work for us, but he approached us with information about your visit to Vladivostok."

Dixon nodded.

"Outrigger, Evergreen," Sydney said over the comm. "She's a little faint. Move closer, if you can."

Dixon leaned forward in his chair. He folded his hands together and placed them on the table near Kai. On one finger, a massive gold signet ring concealed the audio transmitter, which he angled toward her.

On the other side of Kai, Nadia leaned over the table, her low-cut gown slipping down another fraction of an inch. If anyone looked their way, they wouldn't see Marcus Dixon.

"And just who is 'us'?" he asked.

"We are a . . . well, a research group, I think is what the Americans call it. We develop products for specialized markets."

"Specialized? How?" Nadia shot back.

"Our client base is very small. Much of what we do has a very limited application." Kai shrugged, and once more Dixon saw a slight tremor in her movements. "But our clients have the financial resources to make use of our services."

"We understand you are looking for a partner in your current project?" Dixon's voice rose questioningly, seeking verification of the intel they had received.

"It is possible my employer would consider accepting a minority investment—if it came from a trusted source."

"A minority investment?" Dixon drew back slightly.

Nadia was leaning closer, the ruby pendant swinging loosely from her long neck. It dangled in front of Kai like a boom microphone in a bad movie.

"We were led to believe he was looking for a partner," Nadia snapped, "not a fool to be parted from his money." Her dark eyes narrowed. "Let me assure you, we are not fools."

Kai held up one hand, palm out, in a gesture of conciliation. "I apologize for any misinformation that may have reached you. We cannot control the things people will say when they are trying to gain some advantage."

Kai turned her head, scanning the crowd until she spotted Vladimir, who was watching them from the opposite side of the room. "Some unscrupulous individuals stretch the truth for their own benefit, and some have an exaggerated idea of their own importance."

She looked back at Dixon, then Nadia. "But I can assure you my employer prefers allies to enemies, and he treats his allies well."

Kai reached up to brush a strand of dark hair back from her forehead. Her gesture was awkward and uncontrolled. The damp strand remained stuck to her flushed face.

"Is it too warm in here?" Nadia spoke with genuine concern. Kai was clearly uncomfortable, far beyond what might be dismissed as nerves.

"It's nothing," Kai said. She waved her hand as if to brush aside Nadia's question. Once again, her arm behaved like it was only barely under her control.

Nadia accepted her dismissal. In Kai's world, and Nadia's, the concern of a stranger—even of a new ally—was regarded with suspicion.

Dixon leaned in again, sliding his folded hands closer to Kai. "If we're going to be allies, like you say, how about you tell us what the deal is?" Señor Bautista did not consider patience a virtue, or a necessity.

"All in good time, señor." Kai struggled to maintain her stiff posture. "Ji—my employer will want to check your credentials and verify that you actually have the funds you claim."

Dixon slid his hand into an inside coat pocket and withdrew a cylinder. From a distance, it looked like he was opening a fine cigar.

He slid out a slender roll of dark fabric. Inside it was a small handful of emeralds, each one a carat or more in size. Dixon held them in his palm for a moment, then offered them up for Kai's inspection.

She reached out to touch the gems, but her

hand began to shake violently, and she pulled it back. Sweat poured unheeded down her face.

Kai's eyes glazed over, losing focus. Her entire body shook, and she went limp in her chair.

CHAPTER 6

Kai's head fell forward, but Nadia caught her before she could hit the table.

Dixon hurriedly stuffed the gems back into their tube. "Phoenix," he said softly, "we have a problem."

"What is it, Outrigger?"

In the van, Sydney waited for Dixon's reply. She could hear Vaughn and her father reacting, asking for information from their monitoring station back in Los Angeles.

"Our contact has collapsed," Nadia replied.

"We are getting her to her feet, but I think she needs to go to a hospital."

"Bring her to the front. I'll be waiting."

Sydney flipped a bank of switches, shutting down the recording equipment in the van.

She slid the hatches closed, concealing the equipment. As she clambered into the driver's seat, she pulled a lever that unfolded the backseats from the floor. By the time she pulled away from the curb, the interior of the vehicle looked like an ordinary minivan.

Inside the club, Dixon stuffed the tube of emeralds back into his pocket. Nadia had her arm around Kai's shoulders, as though they were having an intimate conversation. She gently prodded Kai's head so it looked as though the other woman was nodding in agreement.

Nadia signaled Dixon, who stood over them. In a single, effortless motion, the big man reached down and picked Kai up in his arms.

The three of them headed for the door.

Their waiter appeared at Dixon's side, worry creasing his forehead.

Dixon dismissed him with a shake of his head. "Just too much champagne." He chuckled.

"We will see that she gets home safely."

The waiter moved away but was immediately replaced by Vladimir.

Vladimir glanced at the stricken woman, then back at Dixon. "What have you done to her?"

"Nothing." Dixon continued marching toward the door, Vladimir nipping at his heels like an angry terrier.

"She was fine when I left her with you. Now look at her." Vladimir stepped in front of Dixon, trying to block the door. "What happened?"

Nadia moved in on Vladimir.

Most of the clubbers had watched them walk across the club, then grinned about the "drunk chick" and gone back to dancing. No one was paying attention to them now.

With one swift move, Nadia grabbed Vladimir's hand and pinned his thumb in a painful grip. He yelped, but the sound was lost in the din of the club.

Vladimir tried to twist out of Nadia's grasp, but quickly found that every movement sent hot needles running down his arm. He gave up on struggling. Nadia pushed the door of the club open and shoved Vladimir out onto the sidewalk.

Dixon was on her heels, with Kai in his arms.

Sydney was double-parked along the car-lined curb. Dixon rushed to the van as Sydney jumped out and opened the sliding door. He lifted Kai into the second seat and slid in beside her, supporting her weight against his body.

Nadia shoved Vladimir into the back. By the time she released his hand, Sydney had the van in gear and was pulling away from the Flowering Lotus.

"What the hell?" Vladimir whined. "What are you doing? You have no right!"

Dixon turned his head and speared Vladimir with a glance. "Don't talk to me about rights. We have a very sick woman, and we need to get her to the nearest hospital."

Dixon could see the mental wheels turning as Vladimir considered his options. "Turn left at the next intersection," he said, choosing cooperation.

"Next left," Dixon shouted to Sydney over the clatter of the engine.

Sydney acknowledged the instruction, and Dixon turned his attention back to Kai, whose labored breathing threatened to stop with each exhalation.

"What is wrong with her?" he asked Vladimir. "She was not fine when you left her, and she got worse real fast."

Vladimir shrugged. "I don't know. She didn't say she was sick, and I didn't ask." He turned to Nadia, as though seeking an ally. "It isn't healthy to ask too many questions."

Nadia gave him a hard look. "Sometimes," she said in heavily accented Russian, "it isn't healthy to ask too few."

Vladimir blanched at the implied threat in her voice. She might be beautiful, but he would be wise to remember the kind of people he was dealing with.

These were people he wanted to keep happy if he could.

"Really, I don't know." The whine returned. "You saw how she treated me. Do you really think she would tell me if she was sick?" Vladimir looked out the window. "Take the next right," he said, "then three blocks and a left. There will be an emergency entrance on the left."

Dixon relayed the directions to Sydney.

They had gone a couple of miles, and Sydney was pushing the van as fast as she dared. The engine raced as she downshifted to take the corner. The three blocks flew past, and she squealed around the corner in a controlled skid. She could see the hospital ahead, and she slowed to make the turn. She slid the van to a stop outside the drab building, under the red neon sign that marked the emergency entrance.

Dixon jumped from the backseat and pulled Kai into his arms once again. She was still breathing, but each breath sent shudders through her body, as though the effort was too much for her.

Nadia followed Dixon out of the van, and Vladimir stayed on her heels. For his benefit, Sydney called to them, "I'll park the van and be along soon."

She pulled away, with no intention of returning.

CHAPTER 7

CITY HOSPITAL #1
VLADIVOSTOK, SIBERIA

The automatic doors slid open as Dixon approached the hospital's emergency receiving area. With Nadia trotting behind him, he carried Kai to the desk.

"She collapsed in a nightclub," he said to the nurse.

Kai took another shuddering breath, reinforcing the urgency in Dixon's voice.

The nurse signaled for Dixon to follow her and headed through a set of double swinging doors into a hallway. On each side of the hall was a large treatment room, divided by curtains into individual areas.

The nurse pointed to the left and ran ahead of Dixon as she barked orders into a radio transmitter clipped to her uniform.

By the time Dixon had put Kai down on a bed, a doctor had come running into the room, followed by two more nurses.

The first nurse grabbed Dixon and pulled him out of the room, back into the hall. Without releasing him, she marched back to the reception desk, where Vladimir and Nadia waited.

"Name?" she demanded.

"Why do you want my name?" Dixon asked.

"Not *your* name, the patient's name. We need her medical history, and we must contact her family." She plucked a folder of forms from a stack under the counter and poised her pen over the first page.

Dixon hesitated. He looked expectantly at Vladimir. He was Kai's contact; surely he would be able to provide the information requested.

Vladimir refused to meet Dixon's gaze. He stared in the opposite direction, distancing himself from the scene in front of him.

Sydney's voice came through Dixon's comm. "Her full name is Kai-Jin Kono. That's as much as we have right now. Marshall is trying to get more."

"Kai-Jin Kono," Dixon repeated.

The nurse wrote it on the chart and looked back up expectantly. "Address?"

Dixon smiled at the nurse. "To tell the truth, I don't really know her. We were talking in a nightclub, and she started acting sick. She collapsed, and I brought her here."

The nurse paused. She looked Nadia up and down, then turned back to Dixon. "Perhaps if we spoke privately?"

Nadia leaned her elbow on the counter. In her thick accent, she said, "My husband doesn't know any more than what he told you. We struck up a conversation with the woman and her date." She hooked a thumb toward Vladimir in a dismissive gesture. "She started sweating and got shaky. Then she passed out." Nadia shrugged her shoulders. "Whatever else you need to know, we can't help you."

The nurse eyed them suspiciously. "You don't—"

She was interrupted by the squawk of a radio

on the shelf behind her. An ambulance, responding to an automobile accident.

She gave the three of them a look that clearly meant, *Don't go anywhere, I'm not finished with you,* and grabbed the microphone.

Dixon stepped away from the other two, busying himself getting water from a dispenser on the far side of the room.

"Phoenix, they have her in a treatment room, but we can't see her. I don't know what's happening. We're going to wait here and hope we can talk to her when she wakes up." He drank a sip of water, then added, "Thanks for the name, by the way."

"Roger that, Outrigger. Raptor concurs. Remain at the hospital as long as you can without causing suspicion. And thank Merlin."

"I will." Dixon suppressed a grin. Marshall had worked his magic once again.

Dixon rejoined the others, and the three of them sat on a bench against one wall. The gold vinyl was cracked with age, and tufts of dirty-gray padding erupted from the breaks.

Vladimir, sandwiched between Dixon and Nadia, glanced nervously from one to the other as silent minutes passed, until finally, he began to relax. Neither of his captors seemed anxious to cause trouble. Maybe there was a way out of this predicament.

Indignation began to build. After all he had done, the only things he had gotten back so far were threats. And where had their driver disappeared to? She said she was coming back, but it had been nearly an hour, and there was no sign of her.

When Dixon went to the desk to inquire about Kai, Vladimir confronted Nadia.

"Where is your driver?" he asked. "And what was she doing there? You were told to come alone. I don't think our mutual friends are going to be very happy when they find out you didn't follow our instructions."

He looked smug, his expression challenging Nadia. It only lasted an instant.

"Little man," she hissed, so low only he could hear her, "I would advise you not to ask those questions of my husband. He is not a patient man, and he does not like to be questioned." She narrowed her eyes, watching the color drain from Vladimir's face. "As for our friends, they should be damned glad we were there. When Ms. Kono recovers, I am sure she will be grateful our driver was waiting."

Dixon returned to the bench, his face clouded. "Medical bureaucrats!" he spat. "They're the same the world over. Won't tell me anything because I'm not family. But they want us to wait, since we brought her in." He sat down heavily on the bench.

In the van, Sydney simply listened. Usually she was an active member of the mission, not the backup. It felt odd, detached. She knew Dixon and Nadia were the right choice for this particular meet. Nadia looked the part, and her accent, though exaggerated, was genuine. Sydney sat back and waited for information from Dixon, or from headquarters, that would determine what she did next.

"Phoenix, this is Shotgun."

Michael Vaughn's voice dispelled Sydney's isolation and warmed her. Whatever their relationship, she valued Vaughn's friendship and welcomed his help. Unfortunately, he wasn't able to offer much of the latter.

She keyed her transmitter, relaying the latest developments, or lack thereof, from Los Angeles to her team.

"Outrigger, Evergreen, this is Phoenix. Merlin is monitoring the Vladivostok police frequencies, just in case there is anything about Ms. Kono. So far, nothing. But we'll keep you posted."

Sitting on the bench with Vladimir next to them, Dixon and Nadia didn't answer.

Dixon wanted to interrogate Vladimir, to dig for intel that would allow the mission to proceed. But they were within earshot of the medical staff, who kept glancing over as if they were checking to make sure the trio didn't leave.

The questions would have to wait.

Dixon looked up. The nurse who had admitted Kai was coming toward them, and she didn't look happy.

"Heads up," he whispered to his companions, and to Sydney.

"Would you all come with me, please." It wasn't a question.

The threesome rose from the bench and followed her back through the swinging doors. She didn't stop at the treatment rooms, but Nadia glanced inside as they passed. In both rooms, frantic activity signaled crises. There were knots of medical staff around many of the beds. Ambulances from the accident scene had delivered four patients on stretchers and two others who had walked in on their own.

Nadia didn't know which bed was Kono's, and she wasn't able to look closely for her before they were past the doors and turning into a side corridor.

It was quieter there, the lights dim.

Without speaking, the nurse ushered them into a small, windowless room. A conference table ringed with worn armchairs took up most of the space.

"Please have a seat. The doctor will be in momentarily," she said, then left, closing the door behind her.

Dixon looked around. The room was stark and sparsely furnished. He glanced at the watch Marshall had given him before they left Los Angeles.

"The Russians are notorious for bugging everything," Marshall had said. "They build the devices into the walls, or the wiring, whenever a building goes up. Now, I know there probably aren't any very new buildings where you're going, but they've been doing this for years, and you're probably going to be bugged wherever you go."

He had handed the watch to Dixon. "Nice watch, right? No. Well, yes, it is a nice watch—leather strap, gold case, would look good with a business suit, or golf clothes, or . . . well, you get the idea. Anyway, it's way more than a watch. If you push this button"—he tapped a tiny gold bud on the side of the case—"it will scan the area for bugs. If there's a monitoring device, audio or video, in the immediate area, it'll pick it up—guaranteed."

Now Dixon tapped the same bud. The date window on the face flashed green for an instant. Clear.

He turned to Vladimir.

"I don't like the way she looked at us," he said. "And I just bet it has to do with your friend Ms. Kono." The menace in Dixon's voice was clear. "If there's anything we should know before they start asking more questions, now would be the time to tell us."

Vladimir shrank back from Dixon's anger. He put his hands up, palms out, in a gesture of surrender.

"I swear to you, I don't know anything."

"You set this up," Nadia said from the other side of him. "You must know something."

"I hear things, that's all. There was a guy looking for money. Whatever he wanted it for, he couldn't go to the banks." Vladimir shrugged. "Some people here thought they might be interested, but he wanted too much money. So they passed the word around. I was at the hotel when you arrived. Figured if I could put you in touch with the right people, you might be grateful. And *they* might be grateful. Always good to have people who think they owe you something."

Dixon glared at him. "So how did you get in touch with Kono? You had to find her."

"You know how it is: You know somebody who knows somebody. Eventually, the guy you want calls you, or he doesn't." Vladimir leaned back in his chair. "Really, that's all I know. I got a call, said a woman would pick me up in front of the submarine memorial."

Dixon shook his head. "We'll just have to wait for her to wake up so she can tell us who her boss is."

But the look on the doctor's face when he entered the little room a moment later dashed their hopes.

"I'm Dr. Belikov. I treated Ms. Kono." He paused

for a moment, then continued. "Did you know her well?"

Nadia noticed his use of the past tense. The news was not going to be good.

"Not well," she said. "We only met her this evening. A chance encounter, really." She smiled shyly at the doctor. "She was taken ill very suddenly, so we brought her to the hospital. It just seemed like the right thing to do."

· Dixon broke in. "You say 'did' we know her. Does that mean . . . ?" He left the question unfinished.

The doctor nodded solemnly. "I'm afraid it does. We don't yet know what happened, but she never regained consciousness. I am sorry."

He waited, as though expecting denials or expressions of grief. But none of them had known Kai-Jin Kono or had any personal reason to mourn for her.

When no one spoke, he went on. "We need to notify her family, of course. Do any of you know who we might call?"

All three shook their heads.

"I see." He moved back toward the door, stopping with his hand on the knob. "I must ask you all to stay for a few minutes. The security detail would like to get a statement from each of you before you go."

He left the room, and they heard a click as a lock turned on the outside of the door.

CHAPTER 8

In the van, Sydney gathered her tools and dropped them into a leather shoulder bag as she listened to instructions from her father.

"We need those medical records," Jack said. "If she had any contact with Jing—and we have every reason to believe she did—there may be something important in her file."

"Understood, Raptor," Sydney replied. She combed her light brown hair back, gathering it into a ponytail. She shed the heavy sweater that had kept her warm in the van, and put on a long-sleeved shirt over her thermal knit turtleneck. It was the best she could do on short notice.

She stowed the monitoring equipment and locked the van behind her. Within a couple of minutes, she had located the hospital's employee entrance.

Two orderlies in faded scrubs huddled under the shelter of the entry awning. The red glow from their cigarettes lit their faces as smoke swirled over their heads and slowly wafted away in the cold predawn darkness.

Sydney strode past them, nodding a silent greeting. She grabbed for the door handle, quickly taking in the 1970s-style security sensor. Without pausing, she started patting her pockets, as though looking for her pass key.

"Where is it?" she muttered. Her Russian was perfect, her delivery just the right mix of irritation and distress.

The orderlies stubbed out their smokes, their break obviously coming to an end. The one closest to her stepped forward. A thick plastic-coated card hung from a lanyard around his neck.

"Allow me," he said, waving his card in front of the sensor. "You should get a cord to hang it from," he said as he held the door for her. "Not as pretty as a necklace, but much more useful."

Sydney smiled her thanks as she walked through the door. "I am so disorganized! My first week, and already I am misplacing things." She glanced back at the other orderly, who followed her through the door. "As long as I don't misplace the patients, I suppose it isn't too bad!"

The orderly chuckled. "Alexi did that a few weeks back, didn't you?" He glanced at his companion, who glared in response. "Supposed to take a woman for X-rays, and ended up leaving her outside the sleep lab."

He laughed. Sydney caught the look from his friend. Judging by the fire in his expression, she may have found the explanation for spontaneous human combustion.

"We all make mistakes," she said, patting the arm of her benefactor. "I bet you are not the only one."

Before the conversation could go any further, Sydney heard Marshall's voice over the comm. "Phoenix, I've got the hospital's floor plan here. Turn left at the next corridor. That will take you toward the emergency room. Let me know when your friends are gone."

Sydney hurried down the corridor, turning

where Marshall had indicated. She glanced back in time to see the two men wave as they continued on their way.

She went another twenty feet down the deserted hallway before she looked back again. The two orderlies were nowhere to be seen.

"Merlin," she whispered, "they're gone."

"Good. Where are you?"

Sydney glanced around for a landmark that would identify her location. She spotted a door with a sign that said RADIOLOGY. "Just outside the X-ray department."

"Okay. There will be another corridor that intersects the hall you're on in about ten yards. Go past that one, then turn right at the next one. That will put you at the far end of the hall from the emergency treatment rooms."

"Roger that, Merlin." Just beyond the intersecting corridor, she found a door on the left labeled LINEN.

Scrubs would be helpful.

She tested the handle. No luck.

She pulled a set of lock picks from her bag and set to work, glancing over her shoulder every few seconds.

Suddenly, footsteps echoed down the hall behind her.

She glanced up. The sound was coming from the intersecting corridor. In a matter of seconds, she would be visible.

With a final click, the lock surrendered, and Sydney slipped into the linen room, pulling the door behind her. She held the latch, preventing it from clicking closed and giving her away.

The footsteps passed the intersection and continued on, fading into the distance.

Sydney allowed herself a quick sigh of relief, then latched the door and turned on her flashlight. The walls of the room were lined with labeled shelves, although most of them were bare.

Empty bins for used linens were clustered in the middle of the small room, ready for the morning shift. She ran her flashlight quickly along the labels on the shelves, looking for scrubs in her size.

She finally settled for a faded green set with pants two sizes too big. She stuffed her overshirt into her bag and pulled the scrubs on over her other clothes. She rolled the waist of the pants, tightening the drawstring as best she could. The shirt was a better fit, though it still threatened to fall off one shoulder.

She tossed her bag in the bottom of a laundry cart and covered it with a layer of rumpled sheets. Shoving the cart in front of her, she left the laundry room and continued down the corridor, as Marshall had instructed. She made the right turn and could see a set of double swinging doors at the far end of a long hall.

"Outrigger," she said, "this is Phoenix. Are you still being held in the interview room?"

In the small room, Dixon turned his back on Vladimir and walked to the far end of the room. Nadia asked Vladimir a question, drawing his attention away from Dixon.

"Affirmative, Phoenix," Dixon murmured, his voice pitched low so it didn't carry back to the curious thug. "No visitors yet."

"I'm just down the hall. Let me know as soon as the security detail is with you. I want you to keep them busy. I'm going to try to get a copy of the medical file."

Sydney continued down the hall, moving toward the nurses' station in the emergency treatment area. She paused in the corridor, studying a bulletin board layered with notices of job openings, meeting schedules, and training opportunities.

Facing straight ahead, she slid her eyes to the right, glancing toward the nurses' station. A woman stood alone at the tall counter, making notes in a stack of files. As Sydney waited, two uniformed security guards approached the desk and talked with the nurse. She pointed to the left, and the guards nodded and moved off.

Sydney moved slowly toward the nurses' station. She stretched her arm out and dug under the pile of sheets in the cart, fishing a miniature camera from her shoulder bag.

She paused again at a drinking fountain and bent over the feeble stream of tepid water. The sharp smell of overchlorination stung her nose and made her eyes water. She stood up, blinking back the tears.

At the far end of the corridor, a light flashed over the door of the left-side treatment room. The nurse bustled out from behind her station and hurried across the corridor to answer the summons.

"Outrigger, are the security men there yet?"

"Not yet. I'll—" Dixon stopped suddenly, then spoke again, loudly this time. "How long are you going to keep us here? We were trying to help that woman, that's all. In return, we get locked in here like common criminals, and told nothing. Is this how your country treats its visitors?"

"Thanks, Outrigger. Keep them busy."

Sydney ran down the hall, the laundry cart clattering over the worn linoleum. She abandoned the noisy contraption halfway to the nurses' station. She could grab her bag on the way back.

She ducked behind the counter, hunching down so that she could not be seen. She stood up long enough to grab the pile of folders the nurse had left on the counter, then ducked back down.

Sydney flipped rapidly through the file folders, stacking the rejected files on the floor until she came to the one she wanted. She stood up again just long enough to return the stack of rejected files to the counter. Unless someone was looking for this specific file, they would not know the stack had been disturbed.

The papers were fastened into Kono's folder with a metal binding clip. Sydney undid the clip and extracted the records. She started at the bottom of the pile, photographing both sides of the page before returning it to the file. The pages were a mixture of medical shorthand and scrawled

Cyrillic characters. Deciphering the jumbled notes would take time.

For now, she just needed to copy the records and get clear of the hospital.

She was about halfway through the pile of papers when she heard the nurse's rubber-soled shoes squeaking on the linoleum in the corridor. Sydney scrambled to gather up the papers and close the folder as the nurse came around the counter and back to her station.

Sydney huddled under the desk, her knees pressed against her chest, the file folder clutched at her side. The sound of her breathing was masked by the rhythmic clicking and whirring of the monitors that tracked each of the patients in the emergency room.

Trapped under the desk, Sydney listened on the comm to Dixon and Nadia arguing with the security guards. They were making it clear they wanted to leave but maintaining a veneer of civility, giving the officials no reason to detain them.

She heard the officers instruct the group to remain in the room "for a few minutes." They needed to consult with their superior, who was due to arrive at any minute.

* * *

As soon as the door closed behind the guards, Dixon checked his watch again. The guards might have activated a listening device after interviewing them. But the green light flashed its all-clear signal.

"Phoenix? Have you got the file?" he whispered.

Silence.

"Phoenix?" he repeated. "Come in. Do you have the records?"

Nothing.

Dixon looked toward Nadia, who extricated herself from her conversation with Vladimir and moved to his side. She wound her arms around his neck, as though placating her ill-tempered husband, and whispered in his ear.

"Where is she?"

"Don't know," Dixon whispered back. "But this isn't good. We need to get out of here and see if we can help her."

"She was at the nurses' station," Nadia said. "We should start there."

Dixon gave her a final hug and released her. "We'll be out of here soon," he said, with a note of authority. "They don't have any reason to hold us."

She nodded and looked at Vladimir. He turned away, embarrassed at having been caught watching their intimate conversation—exactly the reaction she wanted. She smiled.

Another five minutes dragged past with no response from Sydney. She couldn't have been captured; they would have heard something. If the comm was still working, and Dixon had no reason to think otherwise, the likeliest option was that she could not speak without giving herself away.

Finally, the guards returned.

"My superior has given us permission to release you," the taller one said. He glanced at the clipboard he carried, which held copies of their statements.

He turned to Dixon and Nadia. "We have verified your address with the hotel. Please let us know if you make any changes to your accommodations while our investigation is ongoing. We may have more questions."

He turned to Vladimir. "You were with the woman when she arrived at the club, right? We would like to talk with you a bit further before you leave."

Vladimir paled at the request but didn't argue.

Dixon didn't wait. Taking Nadia by the elbow, he steered her through the doorway and into the corridor. The door closed behind them, and the two security guards fell into step with them, herding them back the way they had come and keeping them from lingering in the halls.

As they drew even with the nurses' station, Nadia leaned her head against Dixon's shoulder. "Ready?" she whispered.

She tottered on her high heels, then dropped suddenly to one knee. She heard a tearing sound as one seam of her skintight dress gave way under the strain of her fall.

Immediately, the guards were on either side of her, and the nurse came out from behind her station.

Their attention was focused on Nadia, but Dixon's was not. He was watching the counter from the corner of his eye.

Suddenly, a slender woman in faded green scrubs dashed from behind the counter and sprinted silently down the hall. She grabbed a leather shoulder bag from an abandoned laundry cart and disappeared around the corner.

In a few seconds, Sydney's voice came over the comm. "I'm out!"

Nadia rose shakily to her feet, leaning on the security guards and smiling shyly. "Thank you," she said. "But I'm fine, really." She brushed aside the nurse's questions. "Just tired after sitting there so long."

She stretched, then grabbed the ripped seam of her dress. "I just want to go to the hotel and lie down for a while. I'm sure you can understand that."

From the far end of the hall, another nurse approached. The nurse attending to Nadia excused herself and went back to the counter to exchange information with her relief. She picked up the file folder from her desk and placed it back on the stack on the counter.

Even with that poor woman falling, I really should be more careful with my records, she thought. *The administrator would be extremely angry if I misplaced a confidential medical file, and I don't want to lose my job.*

CHAPTER 9

CITY MORGUE
VLADIVOSTOK, SIBERIA

Outside the aging brick building that housed the central medical examiner's office, Michael Vaughn and Eric Weiss paused for one last review of their mission.

"Tissue samples," Weiss said, "copies of their reports, and simple pictures of the body."

Vaughn patted his coat pocket, checking for the nearly invisible bulge that was his digital camera. "Let's go."

Weiss flipped open his cell phone and made a final call. Once inside the building, they would avoid any monitoring equipment as an unnecessary risk, except in case of an emergency.

The phone rang in L.A., and Arvin Sloane answered. Weiss could picture him sitting in his sleek office, the phone tucked carelessly against his chin as he continued with whatever else he was doing.

"Houdini and Shotgun are in play."

Weiss flipped the phone shut, cut the power, and dropped it into his pocket. This was a simple mission. He shouldn't need to use it again until they were on their way home.

Dressed in off-the-rack suits and button-down white shirts, the two agents looked like mid-level bureaucrats. Vaughn's watch was a Timex, not a Rolex, and they sported penny loafers rather than imported wing tips, a far cry from the stereotype of the rich American doctor.

"Okay," Vaughn said. "You take the lead on this one. I'm just here as backup."

Weiss nodded and led the way up the chipped concrete steps to the front door. A pitted brass handle turned with a protesting grate, allowing the door to swing inward.

The entry hall was poorly lit and painted a nondescript shade of institutional beige. The carpet had faded to approximately the same color as the walls, adding to the general air of depression.

Death touched everything in the building. Dead bodies, dead hopes, and dead dreams seemed to permeate the atmosphere of the building, to seep into the foundation itself.

Weiss glanced down the hall at the signs hung over the doors. The Cyrillic characters were faded, but he spotted one that said "visitors" in both Cyrillic and English.

They passed through the open door into a large room. A tall reception counter ran the length of the room, keeping visitors in a narrow area near the door. On the other side of the counter, desks and file cabinets were crowded into the rest of the room.

A gray-haired woman in a white lab coat sat at a desk directly behind the counter. A sign-in sheet was clipped to the countertop, with a cheap ball-point pen on a chain lying next to it. The woman glanced up when she heard them enter, then went back to her paperwork, ignoring the two men.

Weiss cleared his throat and waited. After a minute of silence, he asked, "Can we get some assistance, please?"

The woman glanced up again, scowled, and looked back at the papers on her desk. "You must sign in," she said in heavily accented English. "Someone will be with you shortly."

Weiss shot a glance at Vaughn, who merely shrugged, and waved a hand at the list on the counter. "You heard her. We need to sign in."

Weiss grabbed the ballpoint pen and tried to write their names on the list. The pen scratched against the paper, leaving a furrow, but no ink.

"Uh, your pen's not working," he said to the woman.

Without looking up, she replied, "Not my pen."

Weiss looked back at Vaughn, who was trying not to laugh at his partner's struggle. Weiss pulled a chrome Cross ballpoint from his pocket, engraved with "Dr. Donald Weaver, July, 1993."

He quickly scrawled "Dr. Donald Weaver and Dr. Eric Cox, Centers for Disease Control and Prevention, Atlanta, Ga., USA" on the sign-in sheet and returned the pen to his pocket.

Weiss and Vaughn waited silently for several minutes. Finally, the woman at the desk put away her papers and looked up. She frowned when she saw that her visitors hadn't left, but she came around her desk and looked at the sign-in sheet.

"Ah, yes, the American doctors." Her tone added *money-grubbing*, even though the word did not cross her lips.

She handed them each a cheap plastic badge with Cyrillic lettering and a metal clip that dug into the lapels of their suit coats. Weiss's Russian was less than perfect, and he fervently hoped the word on the badge was "visitor."

"If you will come with me, Dr. Malenkov is expecting you." She managed to imply that they had kept Dr. Malenkov waiting, even though the two men had been standing in front of her for ten minutes or more.

Vaughn felt like he was back in school, being taken to the principal's office. The feeling was far too familiar.

The woman led them back into the dreary hallway and through a maze of corridors. She stopped outside a windowless door. "This is Dr. Malenkov's office."

She walked away without a backward glance.

Weiss and Vaughn exchanged amused looks. "Sister Mary Catherine," Vaughn said. Weiss nodded.

The moment of levity passed, and both men

resumed serious expressions. There was nothing funny about their mission.

Weiss opened the office door and stuck his head inside.

"Hello?"

"Come in. Come in," a round-faced man with a bushy dark beard called from behind what Weiss assumed was a desk. He couldn't be sure, since all he could see was a mountain of papers, with the man's face sticking up over it.

Weiss waved for Vaughn to follow and entered the office.

"I'm Dr. Weaver," Weiss said, extending his hand to the man behind the paper mountain, "and this is Dr. Cox."

"Dr. Malenkov," the man replied, coming around the desk and grasping Weiss's hand. "I am the chief medical examiner. Glad to meet you, Dr. Weaver." He turned and shook Vaughn's hand. "And you, Dr. Cox." Dr. Malenkov spoke English with a heavy accent.

"We're here about the woman from the night-club," Weiss said. "We are always interested in any unusual viral strains. The more we can study, the better."

"Absolutely," Malenkov agreed. "Our facilities—well, perhaps I should show you what we have here?"

"We'd like that," Vaughn said. "And perhaps we could talk to some of your staff? See what they know about her illness?"

Malenkov nodded vigorously as he led them through a side door of the office and into an adjoining laboratory.

The lab, in sharp contrast to the public areas, had bright, almost harsh, fluorescent lighting. The counters and cabinets were white enamel on steel, and though they appeared worn, they were spotlessly clean.

Two women and a man sat on high stools at different workstations. One woman was looking into a microscope and making furious notes. The other woman racked test tubes as they came from a sterilizing bath. The man was preparing slides of tissue samples. Malenkov went to him first and addressed him in Russian.

"My apologies," Malenkov said to Weiss and Vaughn. "Popov does not speak English. I have asked him to prepare the tissue samples we promised your government and to make copies of the tests we have done so far."

Vaughn decided not to correct Malenkov's assumption that they did not speak Russian. The deception could be useful.

Malenkov led them to the woman at the microscope. He introduced her to the Americans and asked her what she knew about Kono's death.

"Very little, unfortunately," she answered in excellent English as she extended her hand to Weiss. "Katarina Smythe."

She grinned at his surprised expression. "I did my internship in Hong Kong. My husband is British foreign service, thus my name, and my English."

She shook Vaughn's hand and continued. "Ms. Kono was brought to the hospital with an odd assortment of symptoms. Fever, tremors in the limbs, labored breathing. She was treated aggressively with everything the doctors could put their hands on, but it did no good."

"Is it possible," Vaughn began, "her condition was exacerbated by the combination of treatments?"

Dr. Smythe picked up a folder from her workstation and glanced inside, as though refreshing her memory.

"No." She shook her head. "Nothing that

would interact so violently. Whatever killed her, she brought it in with her."

"And have you been able to identify what that is?"

"Again, no. I've never seen anything like it. Neither has anyone else here." She gestured toward the microscope. "Would you like to have a look?"

Weiss nodded. He had little background in medicine or biology, but he bent over the microscope and squinted into the eyepiece and made what he hoped were appropriate noises.

"I have never seen anything like that," he said. That much, at least, was absolutely true.

He looked at Vaughn and cocked an eyebrow. "Dr. Cox?" He gestured at the microscope, inviting Vaughn to have a look.

Vaughn repeated Weiss's charade. His medical knowledge was no better than Weiss's.

Malenkov had listened to their conversation with growing impatience. Now he interrupted Vaughn's examination of the slide.

"If there is nothing more, Dr. Smythe? We should be moving along. I am sure the doctors are anxious to get the sample back to their own laboratory."

Katarina Smythe hesitated, then shook her head. "I wish I could be of more help, I really do. But this is unique in my experience. Perhaps with your resources you will be able to find out something more."

She extended her hand to Weiss. "It was good to meet you. Please, Dr. Weaver, if you find anything, will you let us know?"

Weiss glanced at Vaughn, as though for confirmation, then replied, "Of course. Anything we can do to help both our countries combat whatever this disease is."

"Yes," Vaughn cut in. "Cooperation is critical in medical research." He shook Dr. Smythe's hand and followed Weiss and Malenkov back to Malenkov's office.

The three men made appropriate small talk for a few minutes, with Malenkov clearly delighted with the opportunity to use his English language skills. Vaughn tried to curb his impatience, stifling the urge to check his watch every thirty seconds. So far, the mission had been one of his easiest, and he wanted to keep it that way.

If they could just get their samples and get out before anything went wrong.

Finally, Popov came through the door from the laboratory. He carried a small portable cooler with biohazard warning labels affixed to every surface.

Malenkov explained that the cooler contained the specimens, packed in dry ice. In addition, he handed them a sheaf of computer printouts and a computer disc containing the results of everything done in the Russian lab.

"I hope," Malenkov said, "that this will help you find something soon."

As Popov left the room, Malenkov's voice dropped to little more than a whisper. "None of my staff saw the body, only the tissue samples. I did the autopsy myself." He winced at the memory of what he had seen.

Vaughn took the opening. "Is it possible to see the body?" He could sense Malenkov's guilt over his failure to find the exact cause of death, and he wanted to use that to his advantage.

"Certainly," Malenkov said. "If you wish to see for yourself, before you return to the United States?"

Weiss hesitated, but for only an instant. He had no wish to see something that sent shivers through a medical examiner. But an epidemiologist, offered just such an opportunity, would never pass up the chance, and it was a vital part of the mission.

"I am sure it would greatly aid our research, Doctor, to observe the woman firsthand."

Malenkov opened the door to the hallway. "If you will come with me, gentlemen?"

He didn't wait for an answer but headed down the hall in the opposite direction from the entrance. At the end of the corridor, he opened a door into a stairwell and descended two flights, with Vaughn and Weiss following wordlessly.

In the subbasement, he led them into a cold-storage locker, with a bank of drawers built into one wall. The sting of antiseptic brought sudden tears to Weiss's eyes and burned the lining of his nose. It almost masked the smell of death that clung to the room, despite the clean design and polished surfaces.

Malenkov opened a drawer in the rank farthest from the door and slid out a tray. A woman's body, which was by now pale blue, lay on the tray. She had been a small woman to begin with, and her body seemed to have shrunk in on itself after her death, leaving her no larger than a child.

Dark bands of bruises crossed her body. "She

was convulsing," Malenkov said, indicating the bruises. "They had to restrain her. She was thrashing so violently, she threw herself out of bed twice."

Besides the bruises, there were multiple cuts and scrapes covering her entire body, and clusters of broken and crusted blisters at her waist, armpits, and groin and in every joint. Though her skin was now stark and lifeless, it was clear that the blisters had once been angry red patches, rapidly spreading across her body.

A *Y* incision that had split her chest had been hastily closed with a railroad track of dark, sloppy, and uneven stitches. Her eyes were swollen and matted with a crust of discharge that hadn't been completely cleaned away.

Vaughn reached into his pocket and took out a small digital camera. It looked like any other camera, but it contained some Marshall-designed enhancements.

Vaughn looked at Malenkov and pointed to the camera. "Do you mind?"

Malenkov waved at Kono's battered body. "I have no objection."

Vaughn quickly snapped off a series of photos

from several angles. Although the view on the tiny video screen was exactly what he saw on the table, he knew the camera was performing complex scans and recording X-ray and infrared views in addition to the pictures. He doubted the infrared would yield anything of interest, but he didn't want to miss any possible clue.

Malenkov donned gloves and obligingly rolled the body on its side, allowing Vaughn to take pictures of her back.

Within minutes, Vaughn had the data and it was time for the two agents to leave.

They had already been in the building much longer than they had planned, and each additional minute increased their chances of making an error.

They followed Dr. Malenkov out of the storage locker and back to the stairwell. As he opened the door, Malenkov stopped and turned to face them.

"There is something else I need to do down here. Can you give me a moment, please?"

Weiss and Vaughn exchanged a look. They didn't want to delay any longer.

"We can find our way out," he said. "If that is all right with you?"

"Certainly. Please do not think me rude, but my

old knees do not appreciate climbing those stairs any more than is necessary."

Weiss gave a sympathetic chuckle and shook Malenkov's hand. "Not at all. And thank you for all your help."

Dr. Malenkov waved as he walked away. "Just leave your badges with Magda, if you would. And please let me know if there is anything else I can do to assist you."

Weiss and Vaughn slipped into the stairwell as Malenkov disappeared around a corner.

Two flights of stairs, one hallway, and Magda were their only obstacles, and then they could head home with their tissue samples and photographic data.

No muss. No fuss.

With each turn of the stairway, Weiss felt his apprehension lifting. He had been worried over nothing.

At the landing to the basement, the door opened and a security guard stepped into the stairwell. He glanced at the two foreigners and his hand went to his sidearm.

He barked an order in Russian, flipping open his holster.

Weiss held up his hands and spoke in English. "No trouble here. No trouble. Just visiting Dr. Malenkov."

Vaughn, standing next to him with the cooler of tissue samples in his hand, stopped and waited.

At the mention of Malenkov's name, the guard looked up and down the stairs. He could see that Malenkov wasn't with them, and his expression hardened.

He shouted something at them. Weiss felt a chill run through him. Up until now, things had gone smoothly. But now they were trapped in a stairwell with a nervous guard, who spoke no English.

As time stretched and Dr. Malenkov did not appear, the guard grew more agitated. Vaughn watched the guard's hand as his fingers flexed around the grip of the Stechkin APS. With twenty rounds, he didn't even need to be a good shot.

CHAPTER 10

"No!" Vaughn spoke in Russian, and the guard did an exaggerated double take.

"We are American doctors here as guests of Dr. Malenkov, and we were just leaving," Vaughn continued. He hefted the cooler slightly. "We have medical samples that we are taking to another laboratory. We have our proper badges, see?" He unclipped his badge and held it out to the guard.

The stairwell was not well lit, and the guard motioned the two men through the door into the basement corridor, where a bare fluorescent tube flickered.

He held on to Vaughn's badge with one hand and the butt of his Stechkin with the other. Pocketing Vaughn's badge, he turned to Weiss and demanded his.

When Weiss hesitated, the nervous guard drew his gun and pointed it at the agent. "Give me your badge. And show me some proof that you are who you say you are."

Weiss's Russian was not as good as Vaughn's, and it took him a few seconds to parse the guard's demands—a few seconds too long.

The guard drew back his free hand and shoved Weiss against the wall. "Do not pretend that you don't understand," he shouted, nerves forcing his voice into a higher register. "Show me some true identification."

In an inside pocket of his jacket, Weiss had the much-used passport of Donald Weaver, MD. The pages of stamps were a road map of medical misery.

Weiss reached for the passport, but as soon as he put his hand in his jacket, a flash of panic crossed the guard's face and he lunged at Weiss.

The guard grabbed Weiss's arm and tried to turn him around and slam him into the wall.

Anticipating the move, Weiss spun with the guard. He pulled the guard off balance and twisted free of his grip.

But the man still had his nine-millimeter Stechkin in his hand.

Weiss turned and found himself facing the business end of the automatic as the guard thumbed the safety off.

Weiss stood very still, holding the guard's wide eyes with his own. He raised his hands and drew a deep breath, forcing himself to stay calm.

He spoke slowly and softly, stumbling over the Russian words. "I am a doctor, a visitor. I came to see Dr. Malenkov on a medical matter."

Weiss continued speaking, holding the guard's attention with his quiet voice.

He ignored Vaughn, who was standing a few feet away.

Weiss said only "I," never "we." The guard seemed to have forgotten they were not alone.

"I apologize if I have made an error. If you will let me get my passport from my pocket, I can show you who I am."

The barrel of the gun wavered, then steadied, still pointed at Weiss's throat.

A touch of color returned to the guard's white knuckles as his grip on the automatic relaxed a fraction.

"Would you rather get the passport yourself?" Weiss asked. He wanted to look past the guard, to see what Vaughn was doing, but he resisted. He couldn't risk breaking eye contact.

The guard licked his lips, the pink tip of his tongue flicking across the cracked surface. The nervous gesture revealed how young he was, how unprepared for the responsibility he had been given.

Weiss moved slowly, patting his chest over the pocket containing the passport, without looking away. "My passport is in this pocket. Shall I take it out?"

"No." The guard's voice broke, and he swallowed hard before trying again. "No." It came out stronger this time. "I will get it."

He lowered the weapon, turning the barrel away, and leaned in, fumbling with his left hand for the inside pocket Weiss had indicated, keeping his gun hand as far from Weiss as possible.

At that instant, Vaughn's hand appeared and clamped over the guard's mouth and nose. His other arm snaked around the man's neck. Vaughn was taller by a couple of inches, and he was able to lever the guard back against his body, lifting his feet clear of the floor.

The guard thrashed, trying to regain his footing. His boots squeaked against the worn linoleum, but he couldn't get any traction.

Weiss grabbed for the guard's gun, twisting the Stechkin from his grip and flicking the safety on. He shoved the automatic in the back of his waistband.

While Vaughn held on to the guard, Weiss ripped open the stitching that held his outside jacket pocket closed. From the pocket, he drew a miniature syringe.

With one swift motion, he snapped off the cap and plunged the needle into the guard's neck. Within seconds, the man stopped struggling and slumped against Vaughn, who shoved the limp man against the wall, propping him up and taking the dead weight of the drugged body off his arms.

Weiss took the ring of keys from the guard's leather utility belt and began a swift check of the nearby rooms and offices, looking for somewhere to stash the guard while they made their escape.

The third room on the left had exactly what they needed.

Weiss reemerged into the hallway, pushing a gurney. The plastic covering was cracked and worn, but the canvas restraints were sturdy, and the buckles clean.

Between them, Weiss and Vaughn lifted the guard onto the gurney and strapped him down. He was out cold.

They wheeled the gurney, with its cargo, back into the narrow storage room where Weiss had found it. It nearly filled the small space.

"You okay?" Vaughn asked as they turned out the light and closed the door behind them.

"Yeah," Weiss replied. "But aren't doctors supposed to be exempt from being shot, or something? I mean, we're supposed to save lives. Doesn't that count for something?"

"You have a point there, Dr. Weaver." Vaughn grinned. "Let's get these badges back to Magda and get the hell out of here before they find our friend."

Weiss reached behind his back. "Almost forgot," he said.

He took the nine-millimeter Stechkin from his waistband and opened the door into the storage room. He checked the safety and removed the clip, then placed the pistol discreetly alongside the unconscious guard.

The young guard was going to have a tough enough time when he was found. At least he wouldn't have to explain how he lost his weapon.

APO HEADQUARTERS
LOS ANGELES, CALIFORNIA

Marshall Flinkman stood still in the middle of his crowded workspace. It was an unusual posture for Marshall, who usually thought and moved at slightly less than the speed of light.

He didn't fidget or pace. He didn't speak. He stood a couple of feet back from a computer monitor and simply stared at the display.

His heavy-jawed face was lined in concentration, and his eyes were narrowed. He was completely focused on the problem in front of him, and the twist of his mouth expressed clearly that he didn't like what he saw.

Jack Bristow walked into Marshall's space and looked over his shoulder. Just above the monitor, where Marshall could see it all day, was a picture of his wife, Carrie, and Mitchell, the son that was the center of his world.

The photo reminded Jack of all the opportunities he had missed to be with his own daughter, and he promised himself that he would somehow make up for those times.

After this mission.

Jack turned his attention back to the monitor that held Marshall captivated. Usually the tech genius was anxious to talk, eager to share the information he had ferreted out of some obscure corner of the world.

But not today. Today he wasn't speaking at all.

"You have something for us?" Jack finally asked. It felt strange to have to prompt Marshall.

"Yes."

Jack was becoming exasperated, and his tone was short. "Would you like to tell me what it is?"

"Actually, no, I wouldn't," Marshall said. "But you need to know what I found, which is why I called you in here, and I do have something you should see."

Once the dam had broken, Marshall's words

tumbled over one another, and the torrent washed over Jack as he tried to absorb it all.

"I found a record of Ms. Kono. At least I think it's her; the record isn't complete. In fact, I only found a tiny piece of it, and I'll need your help to get the rest of the file, which is on a secure server at Langley and can only be accessed by the highest security clearance." Marshall cocked his head to one side, as though thinking, then hurried on. "I'm pretty sure I could hack into it—I mean, I know I could, it just might take some time, but there really isn't any reason to, when you have the clearance to just get the file and see if there's anything useful."

"Marshall," Jack interrupted, "why is there a file on this woman on the most sensitive server at Langley? How did it get there?"

"Well, that's the strange thing, sir." Marshall turned to look at Jack, his brow furrowed. "Because you put it there."

"That's impossible. Don't you think I would remember if I put a file on a secure server?"

"No, you did, really." Marshall took a step toward the screen and pointed at a line of the display. "See this address code? It's your ID."

Jack stepped closer, looking at the screen. It

was his code on the file, but the rest of the information didn't look at all familiar.

"When was I supposed to have done this?"

Marshall licked his lips and stared at the screen for a moment, as though something new might appear and explain everything for him.

"It's a file I designed for SD-6 and you stole off the server there. Not that you shouldn't have stolen it," he added hastily. "You should have, since you were working for the good guys and all. But this file, it's a database I designed, and it had intel on Alliance employees and their contacts. It looks like it might not be complete—the file may be corrupted—but if you can get access, I should be able to reconstruct what was in there and get some more information."

"I'll see what I can do," Jack said. "In the meantime, did you find any information in the pieces of the file that you do have?"

"A little," Marshall replied. "I matched the name, and the location code is Japan/Hong Kong region. This is the woman who died in Vladivostok, but I don't know anything else about her."

"I'll get on the line to Langley and get you whatever they have," Jack said. "Just keep me posted if you find anything more."

"I will, sir," Marshall said. He reached for a pair of headphones and slung them around his neck. He glanced over his shoulder at Jack's retreating back, then put the headphones over his ears.

Clasping his hands together, he stretched his arms out, flexing his wrists, before settling down in front of the keyboard. With his difficult task out of the way, he went back to his virtual world, searching for more clues.

Jack left Marshall's office and headed for his desk. He needed to call Langley to retrieve the SD-6 file. There might be nothing more in the file; his download had been interrupted when Marshall had detected his intrusion into the system. But anything was better than what they had at the moment.

He paused near Michael Vaughn's desk, where Vaughn and Weiss were examining a pile of documents, and glanced over Vaughn's shoulder.

A series of photographs was spread across the top of the desk. There was a shot of Kono when she was admitted to the hospital, her eyes swollen, her skin glistening with sweat. Next were three photos of her blisters, the increase in size and intensity readily visible from one shot to the next. According to the time stamps, there were only a few minutes between each image. There were autopsy photos, cataloging and detailing the damage to her entire body, and finally the photos Vaughn had taken in the morgue.

She might have been a handsome woman once, but there was no evidence of that in any of the pictures.

Vaughn was flipping through a copy of the hospital records, struggling with the doctor's handwriting. "Some things are universal," he said in disgust as he examined a series of scrawled characters.

"May I?" Jack extended his hand.

Vaughn handed over the file. Jack's Russian was excellent. Maybe he could get something more out of the records.

Jack puzzled over the hastily written notes for a moment, then looked up. "I think this is about the blistering. Something was spreading while they examined her, fast enough for them to observe it."

Jack pointed to a word. "I think this is 'blister,' and this"—he pointed to another—"is 'spread.'"

Vaughn looked at the words Jack pointed out, nodding. "I can see that now. Thanks."

"Have you found anything else?" Jack asked.

Weiss shook his head. "Everything we have says it's a virus, but the doctors were completely stumped. The notes say they have never seen anything with this combination of symptoms."

Vaughn picked up another file from his desk and flipped a page. "When she was admitted, they suspected H5N1, the bird flu, due to her fever and respiratory distress. That was ruled out postmortem." He gestured to an autopsy report.

Weiss glanced at the photos. "One of the doctors suspected chicken pox, or shingles, based on the blistering, but she also tested negative for that. And shingles doesn't develop that fast."

Jack looked up and raised one eyebrow in question. "My dad," Weiss said. "He had it last year. I read up on it."

Jack nodded. "So we know what it isn't, but we have no idea what it is?"

"Other than a virus," Vaughn said. "We just don't know which one."

"We have the real CDC working on it," Weiss said, grinning humorlessly at the irony. "But they haven't come up with anything yet either. As far as we can tell, no one has ever seen this thing before."

Jack left the two men with the mass of files

and made his way back through the office to his desk. He glanced over to see what Sydney was doing, but she wasn't at her workstation.

The first thing he had to do was call Langley. He fitted an earpiece over his ear and punched in the number for a secure line into CIA headquarters.

His contact assured him the file would be sent immediately. While he waited, he resumed working on his piece of the puzzle: the kidnap victim, Peotr Alexyeev.

The ties between Alexyeev and Kono were tenuous. They both had operated in the Japan/Hong Kong arena. Alexyeev had been kidnapped by Jing, and Kono had claimed to work for Jing.

Were they remnants of the Alliance cell in the Far East, the cell that should have been destroyed in the raids four years ago?

It appeared that ghosts were rising from the dead to haunt the APO team.

CHAPTER 11

Jack spent the next several hours digging into the background of Peotr Alexyeev with little success. When the file arrived from Langley, he forwarded it to Marshall without even looking at it.

He finally managed to find a reference to Alexyeev in Hong Kong, where the man had worked as a geneticist, but nothing more.

Jack worked his contacts, the result of a lifetime spent in the shadow world of espionage. He had colleagues at every intelligence service on the planet, people with whom he shared back-channel connections.

He finally tapped a Japanese contact who recognized Alexyeev's name. "He was brilliant, doing genetic research that could have put us years ahead of where we are. I expected him to lead the way on private research of the human genome, but he disappeared a few years ago. We suspected he was working with the Alliance on bioweapons research, but there was no sign of him in any of the raids in this region."

"Do you have any visual records?" Jack asked.

"Nothing. I did meet him a couple of times, though. I'll get together with one of our sketch artists immediately and see what I can come up with."

"Thanks," Jack said. "Send it to the usual e-mail address."

"I know better than to ask what this is about," the man at the other end of the phone said. "But promise you'll fill me in when the time comes."

"Naturally," Jack replied before he broke the connection.

He had his first lead on Peotr Alexyeev, if indeed that was the man from the police station.

Jack considered what he had heard. If his contact was correct, and if the man in the police station was actually Peotr Alexyeev, he had another connection between the two men: the Alliance. And, if Alexyeev and Jing were linked by the Alliance, they had one more thing in common: Arvin Sloane. Sloane had been a member of the Council of Twelve, with access to the deepest secrets and the most dangerous programs. If the Alliance had a bioweapons program, Arvin Sloane knew about it.

Jack's mouth narrowed into a tight line. Sloane knew more than he was sharing with the team.

Jack's computer pinged, alerting him to the arrival of an e-mail. The message had been sent to an address in Omaha and had traveled twice around the globe through a maze of secure servers and hidden forwarders in a matter of seconds. From Omaha, it had been forwarded through a series of increasingly obscure links and screened through CIA filters before finally arriving in his inbox in Los Angeles.

The message contained good news. There had been a sketch of Alexyeev in the Japanese file. And when Jack looked at the sketch, he had his answer. The man on the screen was a younger, healthier version of the man in the Vladivostok police station.

Alexyeev's identity was confirmed to Jack's satisfaction, with a direct link to the Alliance.

Now it was time to hear what Arvin Sloane had to say.

Jack closed the message, saving it to a password-protected area on his hard drive. He stood up, already rehearsing the questions he would ask Sloane.

As he turned around, he nearly ran into Marshall Flinkman.

"I just wanted to say thanks for getting me that file. Not that it had anything more in it, but I was able to compare the pieces I had with the rest of the file and verify the information I'd extracted."

Jack nodded curtly at Marshall and stared pointedly at Sloane's office without saying a word.

"You're probably busy, huh? Lots to do, and all that." Marshall backed up a couple of steps. "Anyway, thanks." He pointed toward his own workspace and backed up a couple more steps. "I'll just, ah, get back to, um, what I was doing. Okay?"

Without waiting for an answer he didn't expect to get, Marshall retreated.

Jack marched through the workstations, pausing

for a second outside Sloane's office and straightening his suit coat. Then, his posture ramrod-straight, he walked in.

Sloane was sitting at his desk, the tiny boom microphone of his telephone headset poised close to his mouth. He acknowledged Jack's presence with a wave of his hand, indicating the chair across from the empty glass expanse of his desk, and continued his conversation.

Jack sat stiffly upright on the chair. Sloane, in contrast, lounged back in his chair as he finished his phone call and swiveled to face his visitor.

"What have you got?" Sloane asked, his tone relaxed, almost friendly.

"It's more a question of what you've got," Jack said. He looked hard at Sloane. "You knew all along who Alexyeev was. Yet you sent us chasing all over looking for his identity. How much time have we wasted because you weren't forthcoming with this information?"

"Jack, Jack, Jack," Sloane chided. "I never hid the man's identity. I said from the beginning that he was Peotr Alexyeev. I didn't withhold information."

"Alexyeev was an Alliance scientist. He was

part of a bioweapons program. You had to have known that. So why didn't you tell us?" Jack's anger simmered deep within him. He was not given to outbursts, but he also wasn't easily placated. Sloane needed to give him an answer.

"Look." Sloane leaned forward, clasping his hands together on the desktop, a picture of earnest cooperation. "I didn't know it was important. Alexyeev worked for the Alliance for a while, yes, but many, many years ago."

Sloane glanced at his watch and back at Jack. "I have a couple more calls to make, things I am following up that are pertinent to this investigation." His voice was more forceful this time, less conciliatory. "I'm working on this too. And I expect to have some answers within the hour. Would you assemble the full team for a briefing in"—he paused—"fifty minutes? We'll go over what we have and make assignments for the next part of the mission."

Sloane turned back to his computer screen, dismissing Jack. Despite their years of friendship, Sloane occasionally made it abundantly clear that he was in charge of APO. This was one of those times.

Jack didn't take dismissal lightly, but he knew when to push and when to yield. He yielded—for now.

Forty-five minutes later, the team began drifting into the conference room. As each of them entered, Sloane distributed briefing packets containing all the disparate elements they had brought together: the video from Osaka and Vladivostok, Dixon and Nadia's report, the medical records Sydney stole, the reports Vaughn and Weiss had been given, and the latest intel Marshall had uncovered.

When they were seated, Sloane began pacing slowly back and forth across the front of the room.

"Most of what you have in your packets is not new. You have all seen the surveillance videos many times. You've heard Mr. Dixon and Miss Santos's report on their trip to Vladivostok. And most of you have seen at least some of the pictures from the hospital and morgue in Vladivostok."

He flicked his remote control and the pencil sketch of Peotr Alexyeev flashed on the screens. "This is a sketch Jack Bristow got from a contact in Japan. The man is Peotr Alexyeev, the kidnap victim. He is also a genetic scientist who worked, at one time, for a bioweapons program of the Alliance."

Sloane waited for the reactions. He watched the anger and resentment cross each face at the table. Sydney, who had lost her fiancé, Danny, and her best friend, Francie. Marshall, whose genius had been badly misused. Dixon, whose wife had been killed.

He let the emotional tension build for a minute, then raised his hand in a silencing gesture. "I know, I know. How did this happen? How did he escape the raids?"

He looked from one face to another, an expression of concern and compassion on his own visage.

"There isn't a good answer, but I have managed to track down some intel. There was a bioweapons program in the Far East office, BiMedTech." A logo flashed on the screens. "Alexyeev worked there. But the program was unsuccessful; it produced nothing of value, and was shut down as a bad investment long before the raids. The Alliance saw no reason to continue funding a program that didn't produce positive results. The facility was abandoned, and most of the personnel were reassigned to other Alliance offices and projects, but not Alexyeev. He vanished, completely, long before the Alliance was stopped. Until very recently, he was presumed dead. No one had seen or heard from him in years."

He glanced back at the video screens and tapped the remote, bringing up the picture of Alexyeev in his hazmat suit. "Now, it appears, Jing has him."

Jack watched Sloane's performance with a mixture of disgust and respect. The facts he presented were accurate. But Jack was impressed again by Sloane's ability to spin the details to absolve himself of any responsibility, a trait that Jack despised.

"If Jing has Alexyeev, what do *we* have?" Jack asked.

"Not a lot," Sloane conceded. "But we do have the location of the laboratory where Alexyeev worked. I don't think it's a coincidence that the lab was near the Siberian-Korean border, and that both Jing and Alexyeev were seen in Siberia."

"And what are we going to do with that information?" It was Sydney this time, asking the question everyone wanted answered.

"We are going to Korea. More precisely, you and Agent Vaughn are going. I want you to investigate the lab, or whatever is left of it." He turned to Dixon. "Give me a mission plan in two hours. Marshall"—he pointed at the technical whiz—"I want op tech in the same time frame."

He flicked off the video display. "The rest of you, go back over everything, with this new information in mind. Look for anything we might have missed. If you find something, bring it to me, and brief Dixon. Wheels up in three hours, people. I want Alexyeev found."

CHAPTER 12

KHASAN NATURAL PARK
SIBERIAN-KOREAN BORDER

Sydney shifted the high-tech backpack from one shoulder to the other as she stood in the tiny waiting room of the train terminal about sixty kilometers north of Vladivostok.

Dressed in an expensive hemp shirt and an artfully aged pair of denim culottes, with wraparound aviator sunglasses protecting her eyes from the morning sun, she looked the part of an environmentally concerned tourist. A tourist with enough money to afford the cross-country trip on the Trans-Siberian Railway.

She and Michael Vaughn had actually boarded the train in Vladivostok, only a couple of hours earlier. Their conversation was conducted in French, in keeping with their aliases as ecotourists from Brittany anxious to see the Khasan Natural Park, which was located in the southeast corner of Siberia.

The park was home to a wide variety of flora and fauna, and was a popular destination for visitors eager to observe the wildlife, like the Far Eastern leopard, in its native habitat.

Sydney and Vaughn were looking for the habitat of a much deadlier predator: the human bioterrorist.

Sloane had provided directions to the abandoned bioweapons research facility in North Korea. Now Syd and Vaughn waited for the train that would take them to Khasan, just across the Siberian-Korean border from the facility.

Once aboard the train, Sydney and Vaughn settled into a tiny compartment and stowed their backpacks. Syd took off her dark glasses and stared out the window at the passing countryside.

Next to her, Michael Vaughn appeared deeply engrossed in a tourist guide from the Save the Tiger

Foundation detailing the threat to the Siberian environment.

Syd was strongly aware of Vaughn's presence, although she had promised herself she would go slow and let their relationship find its own way. But she had let him get close again, and now she wondered where it might take them.

They rode in silence, each one concentrating on the mission ahead. They had a few hours on the train, then once in Khasan, they had to find a way over the border into North Korea. Sydney wasn't looking forward to returning to Korea. The last time she and Vaughn had been there, they had ended up facing a firing squad.

She hoped this mission would go a little better.

The train pulled into the Khasan terminal, and Sydney climbed stiffly from the coach. It had been a long trip, in cramped quarters. Vaughn followed her, handing down their backpacks before alighting.

As they climbed the steps to the station, Sydney quickly took in the area. The building's exterior was columns of brick, alternating with narrow columns of windows, capped in granite. It sat above the tracks, surrounded by scrubby grass and bare patches of dirt. The concrete alongside the tracks was broken, with large cracks threatening to trip up the unwary.

The small city of Khasan offered little in the way of accommodations, and many of the organized tours used motor coaches or tents. Sloane had managed to turn up a local contact with a motor coach for hire, and outside the station a narrow-faced man with dark hair held a hand-lettered cardboard sign reading M. NOUGUIER. Vaughn hailed the man and greeted him in French.

The man stared at Vaughn, puzzled.

Sydney joined the men and spoke haltingly in Russian. "Are you the man with the bus?" She pantomimed a large vehicle, underscoring her lack of language skills.

The man smiled at her and bobbed his head rapidly, clearly pleased that he could talk to her in his native tongue.

"I am Sergey. Please, come this way. I think you will be surprised by what I have for you."

They followed him around the corner of the station into an overgrown parking lot. There, in all its glory, was their rented motor coach.

It looked to Sydney like a dilapidated school bus. As she got closer, she could see that was exactly what it was. It still had the name of a local school showing through the cheap paint that had been brushed over it. Inside, it had been crudely fitted out for travel. The benches had been removed, and the back half of the small vehicle had a wooden platform covered with a worn futon-style mattress. Underneath the platform, Sydney could see a chemical camp toilet and a battered plastic cooler.

"Pretty good, eh?" Sergey urged, still smiling.

Sydney glanced at Vaughn, who shrugged, and she turned back to the man. "Yes, yes. Very good. Just what we wanted."

She dug around in her backpack and came up with a jumble of papers. "You got your payment, right?" she asked, waving a printed receipt at him.

"No. No money. They told me you would pay."

Vaughn stood beside her, his brow furrowed. "'*Nyet*'—that much I get," he said in French. "But what was the rest of it?"

Sydney rattled back in French, explaining what Sergey had just told her. Vaughn got angry and swore, saying he wouldn't pay the man a second time.

The negotiation continued for several minutes,

Sydney and Vaughn speaking in rapid French, and Sydney speaking to Sergey in slow, stilted Russian. They finally settled on a sum, and Sydney carefully counted out a small stack of bills.

The money disappeared into Sergey's jacket. He thanked Sydney and glared at Vaughn. "Just bring it back here when you are through," he told Sydney. "The stationmaster will let me know to come and get it."

She nodded, and Sergey sauntered away, confident he had made a good deal.

As soon as they were in the bus and away from the station, Sydney dug into her backpack and pulled out a GPS. The instrument had caused envy, but not alarm, when they had arrived in Siberia. Electronic gadgets were the hallmark of wealthy tourists determined to see the "real" Siberia.

This one, however, had Marshall's modifications.

"It looks like a normal positioning system, right?" Marshall had said, demonstrating. "You turn it on, and it syncs up with the satellites, and then it shows you where you are." He paused and looked at the display. "Well, it would, if we weren't in a specially shielded bunker, where the satellites can't see us. But trust me, it'll work. Then, if you turn this"—he flipped the unit over and twisted the power switch—"it transmits your position through a different satellite link, and *we* know where you are."

Vaughn tested the switch. Marshall held out his hand, and Vaughn gave it back.

"Now," Marshall continued, "say you need to disable a perimeter sensor, which a bioweapons facility would be likely to have. You twist the switch the other way, and it generates a variable frequency modulation pattern that can lock onto a sensor and create a feedback loop that will shut it down."

He had shown them the rest of their op tech and given them a pair of top-of-the-line backpacks, a practical choice for the region where they were going. Khasan was short on bellhops and concierge service.

Now Sydney twisted the power button on the GPS, sending a signal to headquarters. She could imagine Marshall or Weiss, or one of the other agents, sitting alone at a terminal, watching their progress as a tiny point of light, crawling across the map on the screen. It was comforting to know someone was watching over them, even from thousands of miles away.

Not that she and Vaughn couldn't take care of themselves. But it was still reassuring to have that connection.

Vaughn drove along the dirt road that led to the park, passing through a lush landscape. Thick stands of oak, ash, and maple lined the road as the bus climbed up mountains and dipped into sheltered valleys. A few miles later, the road left the forest and ran along the rocky coastline for a short distance, past a sheltered bay.

"I can see why someone would come here on vacation," Vaughn said as the road turned back inland, climbing into a stand of old-growth evergreens. "It's beautiful."

He was quiet for a couple of minutes. "Syd," he said softly, "I want—"

"Don't. Not yet." Sydney stopped Vaughn before he could go any further. "I'm not ready to talk about it yet."

She got up from her seat next to Vaughn and moved to the platform in the back of the bus. She sat cross-legged on the thin mattress, organizing their gear for the trek across the border and trying not to think about her relationship with Michael Vaughn.

The sun was setting when Vaughn pulled the bus into a clearing in the forest. While there were no formal campgrounds in the area, the bus conversion was intended to make it a self-sufficient travel home.

The couple exchanged small talk as they prepared their campsite. There were few visitors this close to the border, but they were careful to establish their cover. To anyone happening by, it would look as though the campers were simply off exploring the forest and would return at any minute.

Using the small propane stove in the bus, Vaughn cooked a simple dinner of beef stew, with a loaf of dark bread Sergey had thoughtfully provided, for a price.

By the time they had finished their meal and stowed the gear, it was completely dark. There was no moon, and in the nature preserve there were no lights.

They emptied their backpacks, abandoning the clothes and tourist guidebooks, and repacking only essential op tech.

Vaughn took a pair of snorkel masks from their equipment and handed one to Sydney. Once she had hers in place, he doused the lantern that had provided their only illumination and put on his.

The night-vision masks allowed Sydney and Vaughn to move around the area with relative ease. As they adjusted to the eerie greenish light, they added layers of protective clothing and hefted the backpacks onto their shoulders.

Using the GPS, they silently made their way through the dense underbrush and into the old-growth timber, headed for the North Korean border.

They each wore a comm device, with an uplink to APO headquarters in Los Angeles. As they made their way through the trees, Vaughn reported to Dixon. "Outrigger, this is Shotgun. Phoenix and I are about two clicks from the border, approaching from the northeast. Do you have confirmation on the patrols?"

Dixon answered from Los Angeles. "The satellite imagery is coming in now. Merlin says he can tell you what color their eyes are, if you give him a little time."

In the dark, Sydney smiled. If anyone could do it, Marshall could. "Outrigger, this is Phoenix. Tell him thanks, we just need to know where they are."

"Roger that, Phoenix."

Dixon was silent for a couple of minutes as the two agents continued through the forest.

"Shotgun, Phoenix, this is Outrigger. Merlin advises the border patrol passed your position three minutes ago. According to his projections, they should not pass through there again for an hour and ten minutes. You are a go for insertion."

Sydney nodded at Vaughn, and they quickened their pace. As they drew closer to the border, she stowed the GPS and concentrated on finding a path through the trees.

Ahead, she could see the foliage thinning, then giving way to a barren strip of land, marking the border between Russia and Korea. The trees had been felled, and the underbrush cleared, leaving no cover.

Crossing the hundred meters or so, they would be completely exposed.

Sydney and Vaughn crouched low, poised at the edge of the forest. They exchanged a glance, and Vaughn signaled toward the opposite side. According to their intel, there was a hidden ditch running through the open field, which had been created to stop the local villagers from evading the border patrols. Vaughn took a sensor from his pocket, extending the probe a few feet in front of them.

At his signal, they broke into a trot, with Vaughn taking the lead. He watched the sensor, looking for a change in the density of the terrain ahead.

A warning light flashed on the display, and he held out his arm, stopping Sydney. They both flattened out against the ground and crawled forward, the sensor probe testing the ground ahead. As they neared the ditch, two lights appeared on the display, then three.

Vaughn withdrew the probe and stashed it in his pocket. The ditch was within reach.

From her backpack, Sydney pulled a roll of high-tensile memory wire. She unclipped the bands holding the roll, and the wire immediately sprang into its remembered ladder shape. With the application of current from a high-power battery, the wire stiffened, creating a narrow ladder that spanned the ditch.

The ladder was only a few inches wide, just enough for the two agents to move hand-over-hand along it. The charged wire would hold its shape for two minutes before it collapsed.

Sydney went first, swinging down into the ditch,

suspended above the emptiness below. At the bottom of the ditch, according to their intel, were short spikes—not long enough to be lethal, but dangerous and painful nonetheless.

She worked her way across, aware of the passing of each second. As she scrambled up the other side, Vaughn lowered himself into the ditch and started across.

Sydney steadied the end of the wire ladder as it bounced against the earthen bank with each swing of Vaughn's body. The seconds counted down on the digital display of her watch, warning of the ladder's impending collapse.

Vaughn was four feet from the bank when the charge failed. The ladder went limp, dropping away from the sides of the ditch.

Sydney gripped the wire tightly, bracing herself for the jolt as Vaughn fell. She held on, feeling the narrow wire dig into her hands.

Vaughn was slammed against the side of the ditch, but he managed to hang on to the collapsing ladder. The sensor that he had used to locate the ditch was thrown from his pocket, and he heard it crack against something solid at the bottom of the ditch a moment later.

The sides of the ditch were nearly perpendicular. He tried to find a toehold to wedge his boot into the wall, but only succeeded in swinging himself away from the wall and then slamming back into it.

The ladder slipped in Sydney's grasp, and Vaughn slid a few inches closer to the bottom.

CHAPTER 13

"Keep still," Sydney hissed in the darkness.

Vaughn did as he was told. Slowly, an inch at a time, he was pulled up.

As he neared the top, he was able to grab Sydney's hand, then get one arm over the bank. Vaughn pulled himself over the edge and flopped onto the ground in North Korean territory. But there was no time to rest. They were still exposed.

Sydney reeled in the wire ladder, and they ran for the tree line. Only after they were safely hidden in the forest did she recoil the wire and stow it in her pack.

According to Sloane's directions, the facility was about six kilometers south of the border. Syd and Vaughn set out at a rapid pace, anxious to put distance between themselves and the border patrols.

They moved through the stands of oak and fir, keeping a close watch on the dense underbrush. There were many native animals, and they didn't want to disturb any of them and risk giving away their position.

As they neared the location of the facility, Dixon relayed instructions from Marshall over the comm.

"Shotgun, this is Outrigger. Merlin says you're within two kilometers."

"Roger that," Vaughn replied.

They had decided to wait for daylight before they approached the facility, so Sydney began scanning the area for some cover, where they could wait out the remainder of the night.

A few meters ahead she spotted what she was looking for: a cluster of trees with a fallen log, creating a hidden space. She climbed carefully over the log, testing its stability before putting any weight on it.

The log stayed in place, but the space behind it was partly filled with dead limbs and fallen leaves. Moving slowly, Syndey lowered herself into the pile of branches. It was springy, but it supported her weight without collapsing.

Vaughn followed her over, and they settled carefully atop the cushion of branches, occasionally moving a sharp snag.

Sydney volunteered to take first watch, and Vaughn leaned back against the log. Within minutes he was sound asleep.

Around Sydney, the night was silent. It felt as if she were the only person on the planet. But Vaughn's quiet breathing reminded her she was not alone, and at the other end of the comm link the rest of the team took turns keeping watch on the mission.

When daylight penetrated their hiding place, Syd and Vaughn moved in quickly on the abandoned facility. The compound had once been in a clearing, but the forest was already beginning to reclaim the area. Saplings dotted the field surrounding the building.

Tall gates in a rusting metal fence stood open.

Not that it mattered; the fence itself had fallen over in a half-dozen places.

Even from a distance, the facility felt deserted.

They circled the building, keeping under cover of the forest. It was a plain, concrete structure, with broken-out windows and an empty doorway on one side. The other three walls were blank expanses of concrete, except for a roll-up door on the freight dock.

Satisfied they were alone, the agents approached the empty doorway and entered the building.

The interior had been cleared out. They made their way along the corridors, checking each room in turn, but they were all empty.

Down a flight of chipped concrete stairs, they found another series of rooms. The built-in counters and cabinets suggested this was probably the laboratory. But there were no records, no papers, nothing left behind to tell them who had been there or what they had done.

They moved along the corridors, as they had on the floor above, finding nothing.

At the end of one corridor, a hallway branched to the left. Sydney turned into the short passageway, but there were no doors, just three blank walls.

Sydney stared at the walls thoughtfully. Corridors were meant to go somewhere, not create dead space. But there was nowhere for this one to go, no connection or entry that explained its existence.

Vaughn spoke over the comm from the end of the other hallway. "Nothing here. The place was stripped before they left it."

Their search of the facility hadn't turned up anything useful. Sydney hated to go back to Los Angeles empty-handed. Maybe she could at least find the reason for this strange little corridor with no exit.

When Vaughn entered the side corridor, Sydney was standing against the back wall, running her hands over it. She tested the corners with her fingers.

"There has to be something back here," she said to Vaughn as he approached. "There isn't any reason for this space otherwise."

Vaughn moved alongside her and joined in the search. "You would think so, wouldn't you?" he said, tapping the wall.

Sydney found a narrow crack where two of the walls met. She took a slender lock pick from the earpiece of her sunglasses and ran it along the tiny opening. It caught on something in the crack, with a tiny click of metal against metal.

Sydney manipulated the pick, pulling it back, pressing it forward, levering the hidden mechanism she had encountered.

Vaughn stood with his back to her, watching the corridor. Although they had seen no one since entering the building, there was a small village about three kilometers away, and it was possible they had been spotted.

Sydney bit her lip as she continued to work the pick back and forth, feeling for the right spot. She felt something move and pressed the pick deeper into the opening.

There was a distinct click inside the wall, and it moved out about six inches as the side walls moved outward an inch or two. The back wall angled slightly, revealing a hinged joint a few inches inside, on which the entire wall swung freely.

In contrast to the abandoned and neglected condition of the rest of the building, this door appeared to have been given regular, and recent, maintenance.

Someone had been through this door not long ago.

Syd drew in a deep breath. She backed up a step, sliding behind the cover of the door. Someone could be waiting on the other side.

Vaughn was beside her, reporting the development to Jack Bristow back at headquarters. "Raptor, Phoenix just found a hidden passage out of the basement. It's well maintained and recently serviced." He shot a look at Sydney, who nodded. "We're going to check it out."

"Roger that, Shotgun. Be careful. You should know, I suspect the building is shielded. Your audio is weak, and we aren't picking up the locator. We could lose the connection."

"Thanks for the warning, Raptor. We'll report as soon as we have something."

Sydney inched around the edge of the door, keeping low. The door opened into a tunnel, leading away into darkness. Vaughn listened for a minute, hearing nothing, then signaled her to go ahead.

They moved along the tunnel, which sloped gradually upward. They had gone a couple of hundred meters when they finally reached the other end of the tunnel and emerged at the edge of the forest outside the facility. The mouth of the tunnel was expertly hidden inside a pile of bushes and brambles. Without knowing where to look, they might never have spotted it.

"That's it?" Sydney said. "An escape tunnel? That's all?"

Vaughn looked around but saw only trees and underbrush, nothing to explain the existence of the tunnel.

"We missed something," Vaughn said. "Someone came through that door. There has to be a reason. Let's take another look. Raptor," he spoke into the comm, "we're going back through the tunnel. This looks like it's just an escape route, but we may have missed something inside."

"Roger, Shotgun. We lost your signal completely once you were in that tunnel, so you will be out of contact."

Sydney acknowledged the transmission and followed Vaughn back into the passage.

They had backtracked about fifteen meters, shining their flashlights over all the surfaces of the passage, when Vaughn found a rockfall that looked recent.

When he looked closer, he saw that the rocks

did not touch the side of the tunnel. Instead, they obscured a small opening into a side tunnel.

Vaughn was beginning to feel like he'd fallen through the rabbit hole. There were tunnels within tunnels. Where did they all lead?

Sydney crawled through the opening, dropping to the ground as she emerged in an underground apartment. She waited, listening, for several seconds, before she signaled Vaughn to come through.

Certain they were alone, the two agents made a swift circuit of the apartment. There were three rooms, which may have been intended as a bolt-hole for the Alliance scientists who had once worked in the facility. The first room was a small living room/dining room/kitchen combination. Through a doorway to the left was a bedroom, just large enough for a bed and a cheap wooden dresser.

Off the bedroom was a makeshift bathroom in what might have originally been a closet. A metal dishpan on a tray table served as a washbasin. A chipped mirror hung above it, and a chemical toilet fouled the air.

The agents retreated from the smell and crossed the main room to the second doorway.

In the last room, a small laboratory had been installed. The instruments were clean, and although not new, they were well maintained. While the rest of the apartment was sparsely furnished, with only the bare necessities, the lab was crowded with materials and equipment.

There was test equipment under clear plastic covers, and racks of test tubes, labeled in tiny, precise handwriting. Journals lined a shelf, their spines displaying dates. One lay open on the counter with the test tubes, the last entry only a couple of weeks old.

Vaughn pointed to the date. "He hasn't been gone long. And it looks like he planned to come back." He took a camera from his backpack and started photographing the journal, flipping rapidly through the pages.

Sydney shrugged her backpack off her shoulders and propped it against the wall. She moved into the living area, searching the meager cupboards for any clue to the inhabitant of this strange, underground space.

She found two beat-up pans, a spare propane bottle, and one plate in the tiny kitchen cupboard. A store of canned soup and tinned meat testified to the eating habits of the mystery man.

She went back into the bedroom, her nose now less sensitive to the odor emanating from the bathroom. The bed was a simple platform, not unlike the one in their rented bus. Beneath it were three cardboard boxes.

One box had clothes: a few pairs of cheap socks, some men's underwear, and a couple of plain gray T-shirts. Underneath the meager wardrobe, a flap of the box was creased, and she lifted the edge.

Beneath it, there was a thin layer of papers in a plastic bag. She dumped the contents onto the lumpy bed: a jumble of passports, identification badges, driver's licenses, and a key card with the logo of BiMedTech.

She sorted through the documents, photographing each one. They all had pictures of the same man, Peotr Alexyeev. But each passport had a different name. Two Russian, two North Korean, one Japanese, and an older, heavily stamped one from Hong Kong.

"Vaughn," she called softly. "It's Alexyeev."

Michael Vaughn came into the room and looked at the papers spread across the bed. Alexyeev's picture stared back from each of them.

"It looks like he planned to come back," Vaughn said.

While Vaughn examined the papers, Sydney pulled out the other boxes. One had only a pair of battered sneakers. When she pulled the other out, her breath caught in her throat. In the box was a hazmat suit like the one Alexyeev had been wearing when he was kidnapped.

"Vaughn, we may have a problem."

Vaughn looked at the suit, then back at Sydney, waiting for her to continue.

"He kept this here for a reason." Her eyes darted around the room, as though seeking an explanation. "You only need one of these things if you're working with dangerous chemicals—or something highly contagious."

"But he was wearing a suit in Vladivostok," Vaughn said. "He must have had whatever it is with him. His records should show what it was."

"Okay," Syd said. "You go back to the records, I'll finish in here."

As Vaughn returned to the lab, Sydney started going through the dresser, the only other piece of furniture in the room. She emptied the top drawer on the bed. Nothing but two old sweaters.

The second drawer had linens, which she dumped on the bed too. But as she turned the drawer over, she saw there was a small envelope taped to the bottom.

What was so important that Alexyeev had hid it, even in this hidden, underground apartment?

She examined the envelope carefully before touching it. There were no booby traps, no wires or security devices. It was just an envelope.

She ripped it from the drawer and pulled out the contents: three photographs wrapped in tissue.

The man in the pictures was Alexyeev. It was the same face Sydney had seen in the police station video, without the distortion of the face mask, and the same face that was featured in the multiple passports spread out on the bed.

Each picture showed the man she believed was Peotr Alexyeev, with a woman. As Sydney looked from one picture to the next, she was sure it was the same woman in each picture. In the first two, the woman held a tiny infant, swaddled in soft blankets. She beamed with the joy of a new mother, and a young boy posed next to her, smiling down at the baby.

The third picture was of the couple alone.

Sydney flipped the photos over and saw there were handwritten dates on the back, in the same precise script as on the test tubes.

The two pictures with the children were taken a couple of years apart, and she flipped them back over, taking a closer look. Yes, the young boy had definitely grown from one photo to the other. But otherwise there was an eerie similarity to the two poses.

The third picture, of the couple alone, was the last one, according to the dates. In it, the woman no longer smiled. Her skin sagged, as though it was too big for her face. She looked fifteen years older, even though the date said it was only two years later. What had happened in those two years?

In each of the pictures, Alexyeev had his arm around the woman, and he smiled in a way that was both proud and protective. But Sydney could see a shadow of concern or fear in the third picture. Whatever had aged the woman, it scared Alexyeev.

Vaughn returned just as she was gathering up the photographs. She shoved the pictures back into the envelope and grabbed the stack of documents from the bed.

"I've got the current journal," Vaughn said.

"We can uplink the pictures before we leave so they can get started analyzing them at headquarters. We'll take the rest with us."

Sydney shoved the envelope of pictures into her pocket and stashed the rest of the papers in her backpack.

They made their way back to the outdoor entrance of the tunnel. But as they neared the end, they heard a movement in the brush outside.

Sydney and Vaughn froze in place, listening.

Two voices carried back to them: two men, searching the forest for a lost child.

"Cho? Cho, where are you?" one man called in korean. "When I find her," he said to his companion, "she won't be able to sit for a week."

"Hey," the other man answered. "She's just a kid. Probably was playing and wandered into the forest. You know how kids are."

"Yeah." The bramble at the cave entrance shook, and Sydney held her breath. She tried to inch deeper into the tunnel, but there was a loose stone beneath her foot and she didn't dare move.

The sounds of the men moved a little farther from the cave entrance. Syd drew a deep breath. Close one.

"Still," the second man went on, "you would think she'd stay away from this place. They all believe there's a crazy man that lives out here."

"And they believe there are monsters under the bed, too," the first man scoffed, but there was an uneasy tremor under his words, as though he didn't entirely dismiss the notion. "There have been rumors ever since they closed BiMedTech. It's just a story the kids tell to scare one another."

Sydney listened as the men continued to call for the missing Cho. They moved back and forth along the edge of the forest, never venturing too close to the abandoned building. Their bravado, it appeared, only extended as far as the edge of the clearing.

What had scared these men? Was there actually a crazy man in the forest? Was it Alexyeev? Certainly if anyone had seen him in the hazmat suit she and Vaughn had discovered, he would have looked frightening, especially to a small child.

But if it was Alexyeev, why was he living here, since the facility had closed years ago? What was he doing here alone? There was no sign that there was ever anyone else with him in the cramped apartment.

Were the pictures of his family? His wife and children? What had happened to them?

She could imagine dozens of answers. Knowing Alexyeev had worked for the Alliance, she could well believe he had abandoned them, just as her parents' jobs had made them abandon her. Why, then, did he keep their pictures and treat them as treasured secrets, hidden from prying eyes?

And, most important, why the decontamination suit? What had been going on in that laboratory that made the suit necessary?

CHAPTER 14

The men outside moved away, their conversation drifting back faintly, until it became lost in the distance, and Sydney and Vaughn were alone again.

They quickly scrambled from the tunnel, and Vaughn established a link to APO headquarters.

Over the comm, Sydney reported in. "This is Phoenix. Are you there, Outrigger?"

"Right here, Phoenix." Dixon's voice was calm and reassuring. "Everything all right out there? It's been a long time since your last report."

"We've been underground," Sydney explained.

"We found a living space and a laboratory. It looks like our friend has been living in a secret escape tunnel."

Vaughn signaled that he had established a connection and started the upload. "Shotgun's uploading pictures right now. We'll head back as soon as it's dark. Is the extraction still set?"

"You are go for extraction at 0100 hours," Dixon replied. "The boat will be waiting for your signal."

"Thanks. See you when we get home."

They retreated to the tunnel again and gathered the test tubes, journals, and hazmat suit. They packed them into their backpacks, wrapping the test tubes in clothes taken from the cardboard boxes. Though they didn't say so, they both knew Alexyeev wouldn't be coming back for them.

Once it was dark, they left the tunnel and struck out across the forest, heading for the tiny bay off the Sea of Japan where a boat would be waiting.

As Sydney moved through the forest, her goggles in place, her mind raced. The trip to Korea had provided more questions than answers, and she was anxious to start finding answers.

APO HEADQUARTERS
LOS ANGELES, CALIFORNIA

Michael Vaughn worked silently at his desk. Across the office he could see Sydney at hers. She seemed preoccupied since their return, but she wasn't willing to discuss it with him. She said she was working on the mission and ducked any attempt at a personal conversation.

He didn't have time to dwell on it, however.

Weiss tapped him on the shoulder, breaking into Vaughn's thoughts. "Conference room," he said. "Ten minutes."

Before Vaughn could ask whether it was good or bad, Weiss was gone. Vaughn saw him bend over Nadia's desk, smiling at Sydney's beautiful half sister.

It wasn't hard to see Weiss was smitten, and easier still to understand why. Nadia was smart and beautiful, and she had a basic core of honesty and warmth, just like her sister. What was hard to believe was that such a woman could be the daughter of Arvin Sloane.

Vaughn smiled to himself. If he thought it was tough dating Jack Bristow's daughter, imagine how much worse Weiss had it. *His* girlfriend's father was Sloane.

He joined the rest of the team in the conference room. Sydney sat on the opposite side of the table, between Marshall and her father. While they waited for Sloane, Marshall flipped through dozens of images on the display screens, showing Sydney pictures of his son, Mitchell.

Sloane slid into the back of the room, standing and watching his team.

It took a few seconds for Marshall to become aware of Sloane's presence. When he did, he hastily punched the remote for the display. Instead of turning off, however, the screens displayed a rapid slide show of Marshall bathing Mitchell, the wet, slippery baby eluding his grasp and soaking Marshall in the process.

Marshall punched the remote again, his head swiveling back and forth between Sloane and the pictures on the screen. "Just showing Agent Bristow the latest pictures," he said to Sloane as the screens finally, mercifully, went blank.

Sloane smiled briefly, though his eyes never changed. Marshall's love for his child, even in the midst of a tense mission, was something he understood. It was something he was learning himself, now that he had found Nadia.

But it had no place in this room.

"Please confine the show-and-tell to your own time, Mr. Flinkman," Sloane said, moving to the front of the room.

Sloane turned to face the assembled team, his expression somber. "We have been working on all the materials we have recovered, thanks to Agents Vaughn and Bristow." He glanced from one to the other in acknowledgment. "So far, we have very little new information, but we have found some interesting connections. Mr. Flinkman, I believe you have the details."

Sloane moved to one side, yielding to Marshall, who now stepped in front of the video screens. He keyed the display, his relief evident when the screens showed a chemical diagram and not his son's face.

"This is the latest analysis of the compound Sydney and Vaughn brought back from Korea. We've done some tests, and we know it's an anti-viral agent, but beyond that we haven't been able to determine anything for sure. One problem is that we only have approximately two ounces of the compound, and some of the tests are destructive. We can test it, but then it's gone. And so far, we don't have any way to replace it."

He glanced at his notes. "We know it is a new strain of folded protein, one we have never seen before and don't understand. We don't have any way to replicate it, and we haven't been able to decode its genetic signature. Not that we can't," he added hastily, glancing at Sloane.

"We definitely can, but we won't be able to do it right away. Not like"—he placed his hands on his hips and struck a pose—"Scotty, we need warp engines now!" Marshall turned his head. "I need eight hours, Captain." He turned again. "You have one hour, Mr. Scott."

Jack cleared his throat, and Marshall cut off his performance.

"Not like that. We really will need time to try to find out how this works. All we know, and we're pretty sure about this, is that it was intended to combat whatever virus it was that killed Ms. Kono. That much we know from the journals. Her symptoms are all there. And the dosage is there. It looks like the two ounces we have are approximately two doses. If we're right, those are the only two doses of the antiviral in the world, and we don't know how to make any more."

The mood at the table had gone from amusement at pictures of Mitchell, to somber as Marshall's assessment became clear.

"Thank you, Mr. Flinkman," Sloane said quietly. "Clearly, this is a serious threat."

Sloane keyed the remote. A group of photos were displayed: the police video from Vladivostok, a grainy photo from the SD-6 files, the identification papers and keycard from BiMedTech, and the family photographs.

The faces were all the same.

"As you can see," Sloane said, "we now have concrete evidence of our supposition. This is Peotr Alexyeev, the missing Alliance geneticist. He is the man who was living in the facility in Korea, he worked for the Alliance at BiMedTech, and he was indeed the man at the Vladivostok police station."

Sloane keyed the remote, and a map appeared on the screen, with a series of red dots scattered across the globe. The majority of the dots ringed the Sea of Japan, and there was a secondary cluster around Hong Kong.

He looked at Nadia.

"Agent Weiss and I have been examining medical records," she said. Her accent was slight, but it gave her words a faint singsong cadence. "The spots on the map represent deaths that may be related to the virus that killed Ms. Kono."

A grimace crossed Nadia's delicate features. Kono's death had been brutal, and the image had stayed with her.

"We found a small number of deaths that seem to be linked to either Peotr Alexyeev or Vladivostok or both, all with similar symptoms. Some of them go back nearly twenty years."

Weiss spoke up. "What we found is a pattern of infection that has terrifying implications." He paused and looked around the table. "This virus is mutating, just slightly, with each transmission. We've gone over the records from each of the deaths, and we can see the progression of the disease."

Weiss checked his notes before he went on. "According to recent journal entries taken from Alexyeev's lab, in its current state the virus is not easily transmitted. But that could change. Every transmission, every mutation, is a dice roll. Just once, it's going to come up snake eyes, and we will have a pandemic on our hands—a deadly virus, highly contagious, without any known antidote or treatment. It's only a matter of time. And with our global population density, it will be a catastrophe."

Sydney broke the silence that followed Weiss's prediction. "We only have the newest journal entries decoded so far," she said. "It's a record written by the person who lived in the underground apartment. All the evidence indicates that was Alexyeev, so we're going on that assumption. Whoever it was, he seemed to be infected by the same virus, though it didn't kill him. He kept detailed records of every phase of what he called his 'curse.' In the last month, he noted that it had been more than two years since his last remission. We scanned back a couple of months and found another reference to remission. Apparently that was what he called a period of dormancy, when he was less contagious, but we can't be sure until we decode the rest of the diaries. But he also said he thought the disease had mutated, that he was becoming more contagious, more dangerous."

Vaughn glanced at Sydney and she paused, allowing him to complete the report.

"We think," he said slowly, "that he wasn't wearing the hazmat suit to keep anything out. He was wearing it to keep the virus *in*."

"We—" Sydney started to speak, but Marshall interrupted her.

"Of course! Why didn't I think of that?" He stood up and paced along his side of the table. "It all makes sense. The suit. The antidote. All of it." He was muttering to himself, the words indistinguishable to the rest of the team as they tumbled over themselves, his speech unable to keep up with his racing mind.

"I have to do some tests," he said to no one in particular. He was almost out the door before he turned around and looked back at Sloane.

"If you'll excuse me?" he said, but he was gone before Sloane had a chance to answer.

Sloane spoke to Marshall's retreating back. "By all means," he said dryly.

"There is one other piece of intel that has reached us," Sloane said to the remaining agents. "Jing has been spotted in the Middle East—specifically, in Yemen. He is still seeking partners in his enterprise, and still claims to have a valuable asset, which he refuses to divulge. We suspect that asset may be Dr. Alexyeev, but we don't know precisely what his value is to Jing. Sydney, you and Dixon will be going to Yemen to intercept Jing. Your plane leaves in three hours. Jack will brief you on the particulars before you leave, since Mr.

Flinkman appears to be otherwise occupied."

Two hours later, after a briefing with her father and Marcus Dixon, Marshall approached Sydney's desk. "You were right," he said, the excitement of discovery in his voice. "There were traces of the virus *inside* the suit. We're testing the proteins now, comparing them with the samples from Kono. The difference between the two should give us a clue to the transmission vectors. We'll know how the virus got from Dr. Alexyeev to Ms. Kono."

As Marshall moved on to relay the news to Vaughn and the others, Sydney tried to get the image of Alexyeev, trapped in the hazmat suit, out of her mind. If they were right, and it looked like they were, the man had spent the last two years unable to leave his cavelike home without the protection of his suit, for fear of contaminating others.

Sydney knew what it was like to be alone, isolated, separated from family and friends. Her childhood and her years with SD-6 had taught her that. She had told lies and kept secrets, secrets that had cost her friendships and lovers.

She looked around the APO offices, at the friends and family that now surrounded her. She was rebuilding her relationship with her father, she suddenly had a sister after nearly thirty years as an only child, and she had friends who truly cared about her.

And she had Michael Vaughn. She wasn't sure where Vaughn fit into her life, but she knew he would always be a part of it.

Alexyeev was denied all of that. He was living a nightmare of isolation and loneliness.

He had told the police in Vladivostok he was responsible for the deaths of his family, his wife and children. Were those the people in the pictures? If they were, how had they died? And what role had he played in their deaths?

CHAPTER 15

THE FRIDAY MARKET
SHIBAM, YEMEN

The small airport at Sanaa, Yemen, baked in the afternoon sun. Its exposed parking lot was scorching, even through Sydney's shoes. She wore jeans, a flowing shirt that resembled the traditional Muslim *jilbaab*, and sneakers. She longed for sandals in the heat but kept her feet discreetly covered.

Their car was waiting, parked in a far corner of the lot. When they opened the doors, a blast of overheated air assailed them, and they had to wait several minutes before the interior was bearable.

Shibam, their destination, was about an hour northwest of Sanaa, the nearest airport. Jing had been spotted in Shibam, meeting with potential partners, during Shibam's Friday Market, a bustling, open-air collection of vendors, some with market stalls, some simply tending piles of goods displayed on the ground. It was the last place Jing had been seen.

As Sydney and Dixon drove, they passed rocky plains and small plots of green that were the occasional khat plantations. The road was a two-lane ribbon of asphalt, winding through the barren landscape and climbing the rugged plateaus that covered Yemen.

On a deserted section of road, Dixon stopped and pulled on a traditional Muslim robe over his Western sport shirt and slacks, while Sydney replaced her shirt with a real *jilbaab*, and her sneakers with cotton slippers.

As they resumed their journey, Sydney darkened her face with makeup and adjusted her head scarf to obscure her features. When she was finished, all traces of the tough American agent had disappeared, replaced by a demure woman in native dress.

Dixon parked the car at the edge of the village,

and they continued on foot. Beneath her headscarf, Sydney's communicator provided a link to APO headquarters. A small pack around her waist held a miniature digital recorder, which was linked to a directional microphone hidden in her dangling earring. If they got near Jing, she would be able to pick up his conversation without detection.

Walking a few steps ahead of her, Dixon wore aviator-style sunglasses. In addition to shielding his eyes from the intense sun, they concealed a digital camera with telephoto capability. Even at a distance of a hundred yards, he could photograph Jing and his companions.

The two agents made their way through Shibam, moving along the dirt streets toward the market. Along the narrow roads, buildings of stone and dun brick rose several stories into the air, their arched windows open to the desert breeze. Near the center of the town, a minaret towered over the surrounding buildings, decorated with an ornate filigree of darker brown.

As they neared the market, the crowds grew increasingly dense, until Dixon and Sydney became part of a solid mass of people, milling about in the small square.

They threaded their way among the shoppers and vendors, watching for Jing. According to their intel, he frequented a coffee vendor on one side of the market, and they headed in that direction. It was as good a place as any to start.

As Sydney wandered through the market, her eyes darting from one face to the next, always look-ing for Jing, she wished she could stop and exam-ine the goods for sale. Her gaze slid over a display of colorful robes, exotic fabrics that would be beau-tiful on her sister.

There wasn't time to stop. Maybe someday she would. But right now she was looking for a terrorist, a man who threatened the world.

She remembered the look on Alexyeev's face as Jing had dragged him from the police station in Vladivostok. He had been frightened, terrified of Jing and his troops. She continued scanning the crowd and listening for a signal that Dixon had spotted their quarry.

Her comm remained silent as they neared the coffee shop.

She was within ten yards of it when she saw him. Standing next to the folding table that served as a counter, he held a glass tumbler of black coffee in a brass cradle. He was turned away from her, only his profile visible, but she was certain it was Jing.

"Got him, Outrigger," Sydney said quietly. "At the left end of the coffee shop."

"I see him, Phoenix, and I'm getting pictures now," Dixon replied. "Can you hear anything?"

Sydney adjusted the fanciful earring that dangled from her right ear, paused for a moment, then fiddled with it again. "Negative, Outrigger. I think I'm too far away."

She started moving closer, inching past the adjacent stall and pretending to examine the brass pots displayed there.

She had covered about half the distance to Jing when another man joined him. The two men greeted each other warmly, as though they were old friends, and together they walked off into the crowd.

"He's moving," Sydney said. She dropped the pot she was holding and headed through the crowd after Jing and his companion. They were soon swallowed up by the press of bodies, and she lost sight of them.

"Outrigger! I've lost visual contact. Do you have them?"

"Next to the baker," Dixon replied. "He's buying bread and talking a mile a minute. Can you get close enough to hear?"

Sydney slid through the crowd. Her *jilbaab* swirled around her as she twisted and turned, making her way to the baker's stall, where Jing was haggling about the cost of his purchase. She turned her head slightly, angling the microphone toward the stall. The argument continued for a couple of minutes, with Jing bullying the vendor well beyond the acceptable limits of negotiation.

He was a man who took whatever he could.

Jing finally paid the vendor far less than the bread was worth and moved on. Sydney trailed after the two men, staying as close as she dared. Dixon moved parallel to her path, keeping the three of them in sight. The two men wandered the market, stopping occasionally to finger a display of goods before moving on. They acted as though they had all the time in the world.

Jing and his companion reached a stall at the edge of the market and suddenly turned away from the crowd, moving through the narrow streets.

Dixon tried to follow, but his path was blocked by a food cart with a glowing brazier balanced precariously on top. As he tried to dodge around the cart, the vendor grabbed his robe and began yelling at him to be careful, he could start a fire. Other vendors and shoppers in the crowd joined in, berating Dixon for his carelessness.

Sydney, hearing the commotion, detoured around the escalating argument. Dixon would have to take care of himself for the moment. Her attention was focused on the escaping targets.

Jing broke into a run, putting distance between himself and the market. He dodged down an alley, his companion running alongside him.

Sydney ran behind them, stealth sacrificed for speed. She cursed under her breath as a sharp pebble dug into her foot through the thin cotton of her slipper, but she didn't slow her pace.

Over the comm, she could hear Dixon apologizing to the vendor. His soft-spoken charm was working, and behind her the angry buzz of the crowd dissipated.

But Dixon was too far away to help her now.

She ran after the two men, dodging around children in the street. A young boy led a donkey from its stable under a house as she rounded a corner. She couldn't slow down, and she flew past the startled animal, setting it to braying loudly.

Jing and his companion had reached the edge of the village, and they began scrambling up the steep cliff behind it.

Caves riddled the cliff face. On the lower reaches, narrow buildings, like those in town, clung to the side of the cliff. Loose rocks rattled down as the men clambered up. Behind them, Sydney started climbing, her *jilbaab* catching on the prickly cacti that covered the lower levels. She yanked the fabric loose, scrambling higher.

"Outrigger, he's headed for the caves."

"Almost there, Phoenix."

She glanced up, catching movement off to her left. She moved in that direction, feeling for a handhold while keeping Jing in sight.

The two men drew level with a cave opening.

"Right behind you, Phoenix," Dixon said over the comm. "I'm coming up."

Sydney fought the impulse to turn and look for Dixon. She had to keep her eyes on Jing.

Above her, Jing paused as the other man ducked into the cave. He stooped and came up with two large rocks in his hands. With a careless flick of his wrist, he set the rocks tumbling down the cliff.

The rocks dislodged stones and dirt as they accelerated down the hillside, raining debris on Sydney. She ducked, covering her head with her hands as the shower of rocks crashed around her. A large stone slammed into her shoulder, sending a dagger of pain along her arm and back. Another, sharper one bit into the exposed flesh of her arm. A warm stream ran down to her elbow. She was bleeding, but she couldn't look at the wound until the hail of stones stopped.

By the time the small avalanche passed, Dixon had caught up with her. He reached for her arm, but she pulled away and started climbing again.

"I saw where they went. We can't let them get away."

Dixon nodded and followed her up the side of the cliff.

They found the cave where Jing had disappeared. Sydney stopped beside the entrance and ripped away the lower part of the *jilbaab*.

Sydney and Dixon produced .357 Sig Sauer automatics, and thumbed off the safeties. They paused at the entrance to the cave, listening for Jing.

Deep within the cave, there was the hollow

echo of running feet. Sydney lunged into the mouth of the cave and flattened herself against the wall. She didn't hesitate, knowing she would be a target silhouetted in the light from the outside if she did.

No one shot at her or came at her out of the dark. After a few seconds, Dixon followed her in.

Together, they made their way into the darkness, feeling their way along. After about twenty feet, the cave widened into a small room.

The only sound was a distant rattle of stones, as though someone had set off another small avalanche.

Dixon switched on a narrow-beam flashlight and played it over the walls of the cave.

As they watched with sinking hearts, Sydney and Dixon saw the awful truth: There were at least five separate tunnels leading away from the space where they stood, and they were all silent.

Jing could have taken any one of them, and Dixon and Sydney had no way of knowing which.

Sydney muttered a curse as Dixon pulled back her sleeve to examine the wound on her arm. They had lost Jing.

CHAPTER 16

APO HEADQUARTERS
LOS ANGELES, CALIFORNIA

"Mr. Bristow?" Marshall Flinkman hesitated, a few feet from Jack's desk, a laptop clutched against his chest. "You asked me to let you know if I found something."

Marshall shifted his weight from one foot to the other, but he didn't come any closer. The truth was, Jack Bristow made him more nervous than any professor at Cal Tech ever had.

Although they had worked together for years and Marshall knew Jack respected his technical expertise, the older man was intimidating. There was a stillness, a motionless silence about him, that made Marshall uneasy.

"And have you? Found something?"

"Yes." Marshall moved closer and glanced furtively around, as though afraid someone might overhear their conversation. "It's about the Alliance," he whispered.

Jack got up from his desk and stood next to Marshall. "Perhaps," he said, looking at the laptop Marshall clutched, "you would like to show me what you have."

Marshall followed Jack into a small meeting room and closed the door behind him. He set the laptop on the table and called up a file with a few keystrokes.

"What I have," he said, "is from the SD-6 file you retrieved from Langley. You know, the one you stole from me when—well, not so much stole, as copied, and . . . anyway"—he paused to gather his thoughts—"that file had a bunch of Alliance correspondence."

He tapped the keyboard, displaying an exchange of electronic messages between members of the Alliance of Twelve.

"Here." He turned the laptop toward Jack,

pointing at a specific series of messages. "These are from Alain Christophe and Karl Dryer. They're talking about other Alliance officers. They think— well, you can see what they think."

"They suspect some of the officers of trying to develop their own networks, independent of the Alliance." Jack swiveled his head toward Marshall. "But they didn't know who they were?"

Jack kept his face impassive. He knew Sloane had been guilty of exactly such duplicity. Had Marshall found some evidence implicating Sloane?

"Now, this," Marshall continued, "is where it gets interesting." He scrolled through the file until he found the spot he was looking for.

"Here is where Dryer names some of the people he thinks are involved. Most of these are the names of people we know died in the raids, or who were captured. But here"—he indicated a message on the screen—"here's the name we're looking for: Gai Dong Jing."

Jack read through the message Marshall indicated and the exchange that followed. Jing was under investigation within the Alliance just before the raids. He was suspected of having a private agenda.

But there was no mention of Sloane, no suspicion that he was manipulating the Alliance to his own benefit. Jack was relieved; they didn't need the distraction of four-year-old accusations muddying the waters while they searched for Jing.

"Did you find anything else?" Jack asked. The file was extensive, and he was certain Marshall had already discovered whatever helpful intel it contained.

"Actually, there was one more thing. Christophe tells Dryer to add the name of Abdul Kamal to his investigation. He and Jing were close friends, and Christophe said that anything Jing was involved with, Kamal was too."

"Where do we find Abdul Kamal?" Jack asked.

"Well, that's the thing. I checked the records from the raids. Kamal is listed as missing in the reports from the raids in Afghanistan. They never positively identified his body. But he had a friend, a woman who worked in the Afghan station. Rumor has it they were more than friends, if you know what I mean," Marshall said.

Jack just stared at him, expressionless, and Marshall hurried on. "She was captured and is in prison in Kandahar. There was always some suspicion that some of the Afghan records weren't destroyed, but she's never been willing to talk."

"What makes you think we can change her mind?"

"There's a growing movement to reinstate the death penalty in certain cases. Hers is one of them."

Jack stood up. "It looks like we need a team in Kandahar."

CENTRAL PRISON
KANDAHAR, AFGHANISTAN

The woman sitting across the battered wooden table in the prison interrogation room was not what Sydney had expected. She had expected the sunken eyes, hollow cheeks, and stringy hair. It was no surprise that her hands were rough and her arms and legs were as thin as a child's. Poor nutrition and lack of exercise had sapped her strength and her will.

What Sydney hadn't expected was the blonde hair and blue eyes, and the suggestion, despite the abuse, that her skin had once been fair and dewy.

The records on Changaze Dabu had been sparse. There were only a few grainy, long-lens photographs from her trial, showing a slender figure in a burka, her hair and features obscured by the traditional head scarf and veil that was the only acceptable costume for an Afghan woman.

"What do you want from me?" she asked. Her voice was sullen, a mixture of defensiveness and challenge. She tried to appear tough, to act as if she didn't need anyone. But the soft, upper-crust British accent betrayed her.

This was a woman born to wealth and privilege. Whatever had led her to her position with the Alliance, it had clearly turned out very different from what she had anticipated.

Fear shadowed her eyes. She knew her life was in danger, that her death sentence might be reinstated at any time. The bravado was a thin veneer over the panic she struggled to hide.

"A better question," Sydney said softly, "is what can we do for you?"

"Nothing. There is nothing anyone can do for me." Bitterness suffused her words. She expected to spend the rest of her life, however short it might be, in the hell that was an Afghan prison, and she refused to hope for anything else.

"That's where you're wrong," Dixon said,

pulling a sheaf of papers from the briefcase he carried. "There is a great deal we can do for you, starting with saving your life."

"Look around," Dabu waved one matchstick-thin arm, indicating the shabby room and the prison outside it. "That isn't a real bonus."

"It is," Sydney said, "if you aren't here."

"Oh, yeah." Sarcasm dripped from Dabu's words. "They're going to just let me waltz out of here and go back to London, where they'll welcome me with open arms."

"Not London," Sydney said, "but we can offer you asylum in the United States. Unless"—she paused and looked pointedly at their surroundings—"you'd rather stay here."

A glimmer of hope flashed across Dabu's face, then vanished as quickly as it had appeared. She knew better than to allow herself to be optimistic.

"It's true," Dixon said, pushing the papers across the table to her. "We have the authority of the United States government to offer you placement in the federal Witness Protection Program. You'll be provided a new identity, a job, and a place to live—the opportunity to start a new life, to have a life, not a life sentence."

Dabu reached out a shaky hand, pulling the stack of papers nearer. She looked at the top page, then carefully lifted it close to her face, squinting to bring the words into focus.

She read for several minutes, lifting each page separately and laying it upside down on the table as she finished.

Sydney and Dixon waited silently. It was like trying to tame an animal that had been abused. They had to let her trust them first. She had taken the bait, but they had to be patient and let her come to them.

Dabu read through the stack and sat staring at the tabletop for several minutes more. Her internal struggle was clear, as hope and fear battled for control. These American strangers appeared to be throwing her a lifeline.

Could she trust them?

Her face softened for a moment, and a faint smile tugged at the corners of her mouth. It was as if she allowed herself to remember what it was like to live outside the walls of a prison, to be able to move about freely, to have enough to eat.

Her eyes focused again on her surroundings, and despair took control once again. She didn't—couldn't—dare to believe them.

Sydney saw the opportunity slipping away. Dabu refused to hope, and without hope, there would be no trust. She would spend the rest of her life in isolation, locked behind the walls of the stone prison.

"You have no reason to trust us," Sydney said. She kept her voice low and soothing. "I know that. I understand that. Everyone you trusted has betrayed you, raised your hopes only to abandon you."

Sydney stretched her hand across the table, resting it lightly against the cracked knuckles of Dabu's hand. "But we do want to help you, if you'll let us. You don't have to take our word for it; you have it in writing."

Dabu glanced again at the stack of papers. Sydney willed herself to remain motionless and let Dabu come to her.

At last, slowly, hesitantly, Dabu looked up, a glimmer of hope in her eyes. "What would I have to do?"

Syd resisted the temptation to smile. They didn't have the information—yet. But the first step had been taken.

"The papers say you'll do this in 'consideration'

of my 'assistance.' But I don't know what that assistance is."

"You were, uh, friends," Dixon said, "with a man named Abdul Kamal. You worked together here in Kandahar a few years ago. Kamal was an associate of a man we are looking for, Gai Dong Jing."

Dabu cringed at the mention of Kamal's name. Pain and loss twisted her features and brought tears to her eyes, confirming the rumors. They had definitely been more than friends—much more.

Syd felt a wave of sympathy for the other woman. Whatever Abdul Kamal had been, she had loved him, and he was gone. Syd remembered losing Danny, and the searing pain that had nearly consumed her. It was the same pain she saw on Dabu's face, magnified by the terror and isolation of prison.

"Tell us what you know about Kamal and Jing. Help us, and we'll help you."

Dixon spoke with the calm authority of a man used to being obeyed, giving Dabu a final push. The tears spilled over, trickling down the hollows of her cheeks and dripping unheeded from her chin.

"They killed him." She struggled a moment,

then continued. "He's gone, and I will never see him again in this life."

She blinked rapidly, stopping the flow of tears, but the dam had been breached, and she couldn't stop the words that rushed from her mouth in a torrent.

"He was more than a friend," she said. "But I think you already knew that. That's the real reason I am here. Not for the job I did. I was just a file clerk who didn't know anything about their operation. I'm in here because the authorities were trying to curry favor with the West. The sentence the prosecutor wanted was death by stoning, for being Abdul's lover." She shuddered at the thought of what had nearly happened.

"But the publicity that would have come from executing a British divorcée was more than the local mullah was willing to risk. So I was charged with espionage and sentenced to life in this hellhole. They wanted me to betray Abdul, just as you do. And they offered all kinds of deals, but I didn't trust them to keep their word. And you couldn't tell from one week to the next who was actually in charge."

"This time," Dixon assured her, "we have the

backing of the man in charge right this minute. It may change," he conceded, "but for today, we have your pardon in hand—if you want it."

"I didn't think I would," Dabu said. "But I don't want to die, especially not here. I want to be Charlene again—that was my English name, before I adopted an Afghan one—and live with people I can talk to. I don't want to keep secrets anymore." Her bitter tone returned for a moment. "They never did do me much good. Maybe they'll help you."

Dabu held out her hand to Dixon, who unclipped the pen from his pocket and handed it to her. She signed the pardon offer with a flourish, first in Arabic, then, with a forceful hand, she added "Charlene Davies" in elegant Spencerian script.

She looked up at Sydney and smiled for the first time. "They taught us that in boarding school. A proper lady always has a fine hand."

Sydney smiled back. "I'm glad you decided to trust us."

"So, now," Dabu began, "what do we do?"

"First, we get you out of here." Dixon rose from his chair and knocked on the door. When the guard appeared, Dixon spoke to him briefly. The man nodded and disappeared. He reappeared in a couple of minutes accompanied by the warden of the prison.

Dabu sprang to her feet when the man entered the room, unable to control her response. He waved her back into her chair, and her eyes widened as she finally allowed herself to believe her good fortune.

It took less than an hour to process her release, and soon she was in a car with Sydney and Dixon, heading for a CIA safe house on the outskirts of the city.

Dixon left Sydney and Charlene, as she had asked them to call her, at the safe house, while he made a foray into the open-air market a couple of miles away.

He took his time walking among the stalls, looking over the selections. Charlene had seemed comfortable with Sydney, and he was deliberately leaving them alone.

There were guards watching the house, of course. Afghanistan was in turmoil, and dramatic power shifts were a fact of life.

He stopped at a dried fruit stand for dates and raisins, then a few steps later he added fresh-baked naan to his shopping basket. Some pomegranate juice, a little cheese, and he had a solid meal for their latest ally.

When he returned to the house, the two women were talking intently, sitting in matching armchairs in the small living room. He went directly to the kitchen, where he assembled the food and a pot of hot tea.

By the time the food was ready, the conversation in the living room had stopped. He carried the tray quietly into the room, placing it on a low table in front of Charlene.

"I thought you might be hungry," he said.

Charlene was exhausted. The battling emotions of the morning had left her drained. Her eyelids drooped, but she looked up at Dixon with a grateful smile.

"That's more food than I have seen in a month," she said. "Thank you."

"Tea?" Dixon handed her a ceramic mug. "I'm afraid we don't have proper cups."

Charlene tested the heat of the brew, sipping experimentally, then gave a satisfied sigh. "It's perfect. I haven't had a good cup of tea in years."

While Charlene ate, Sydney filled Dixon in on

what she'd learned while he was gone.

"The Alliance was right about Kamal," she told him. "He was keeping a set of private files, files his Alliance superiors had begun to suspect he had. He figured he could use them to buy his way out when he was ready to leave. He told Charlene"— she nodded at the woman who was piling cheese on a piece of naan—"that they would go away together."

"Where did he keep the files?" Dixon interjected. "The facilities here were destroyed, and we haven't been able to find any sign of another location."

"Not here," Sydney said. "Not even in Afghanistan. He gave them to an ally for safekeeping and was killed before he had a chance to retrieve them. They're in the hands of Kamal's friend, Abaas Abdullah. He's chief of a remote tribe in Eygypt's Blue Desert."

Dixon thought for a minute, then looked at Charlene. "Are you ready to travel? I think we should get out of here as soon as possible."

She squeezed her temples, then rubbed her eyes. With the last of her reserves, she rose from her chair and looked from Dixon to Sydney. "We cannot leave this godforsaken place soon enough to please me."

Charlene set her empty mug on the table and picked up the small linen sack that contained all her worldly goods. Even in her weakened state, it wasn't a strain for her to carry it.

"Ready when you are."

CHAPTER 17

THE BLUE DESERT
SINAI PENINSULA

Sydney urged her camel forward. She felt as though she had been riding forever, though it had been only a few hours. Dressed in men's robes, her face was uncovered, with an artfully applied shadow of beard spread across her cheeks and chin.

Under her robes, her slight, athletic body had been wrapped in a tight bodysuit, giving her the appearance of a slender young man.

Beside her, Dixon shifted in his saddle, a vain attempt to make himself comfortable. His left leg, wrapped around the horn of the tall saddle, was developing a cramp.

"Tell me again why we didn't take a Jeep," Dixon said.

"Because Abdullah is camped in a rocky area. Nothing with tires could get close. Besides," she teased, "aren't you having fun?"

Dixon wiggled a little and settled himself. "There are many things I would call this. Fun is not one of them."

Sydney pushed her sleeve back and consulted the miniature GPS monitor strapped to her wrist. To the casual observer, it appeared to be a cheap dime-store watch. But when the stem was pulled out, a sophisticated GPS display pinpointed their location.

"Not far now, if our intel is correct," she said, scanning the horizon.

The sun was high as they crossed the open expanse of the desert, and they were approaching a series of low hills, their sides covered with rocks and small boulders.

The camels picked their way confidently between the rocks, placing their wide feet in the exact right spot to maintain their steady, rocking gait.

Syd's camel started down a narrow canyon, with Dixon behind her. The GPS indicated they were moving in the right direction, and the camel seemed familiar with the route.

They moved deeper into the canyon. Syd could feel the hair on the back of her neck rising. They were in unknown territory, without backup.

The camels slowed as they picked their way through the tumbled rocks.

From behind them, Sydney heard stones rattle. She turned in her saddle. Beyond Dixon, three men on camels appeared. Syd realized they had come out from behind one of the hills, but she couldn't shake the feeling that the men had simply materialized out of the desert.

The leader of the men shouted at her to stop, then issued a harsh command to her camel, which instantly pulled up and waited for the men to approach.

The men circled around her and Dixon, staring them up and down. The leader smiled at Sydney, his white teeth a sharp contrast to the leathery darkness of his sun-dried skin.

The phrase "undressing her with his eyes" flashed through her mind as she waited for the man to speak. Would he see past her disguise? Or perhaps young men were his taste.

She kept her posture tall and proud, daring him to challenge her.

"Come with us," he said at last, turning away.

"Why should we?" Sydney kept her voice pitched low, her tone quiet but firm. She didn't want a confrontation, but neither did she want to follow his demands without protest.

"Because you want to see Abaas Abdullah."

The man rode ahead of her, his companions following him. Sydney and Dixon exchanged a look, and Dixon shrugged as they fell into line behind the riders.

Sydney's comm link sputtered, and Dixon's voice came softly into her ear. "Well, we want Abdullah, and they seem to know it, so we might as well follow them."

"I agree," Sydney said, "especially since the camels seem inclined to do whatever he tells them."

As they rode, Dixon mentally cataloged the weapons concealed beneath his robes. Both he and Sydney were well armed if a fight became necessary.

They had heard stories of treacherous guides and bold thieves who robbed tourists and left them stranded in the desert. But these men knew they were looking for Abdullah, and they weren't treating them like captives or hostages.

Still, the heft of an automatic weapon was reassuring, and the sword he wore strapped at his side, although its function was mostly decorative, was well balanced and carried a razor-sharp blade.

He hoped he wouldn't have to use either one.

The agents followed the men through the narrow valley and out the other side. They passed a small oasis, then continued on through the desert.

They passed through a section of desert where the rocks were bright blue. Sydney could see that the coat of paint was chipping and flaking in places, but the effect was still startling. In the middle of the dun desert and red-orange cliffs, rocks the color of the sky turned the world upside down.

They rode on as the sun dipped low and the heat of the day gave way to cool and then cold of night.

Stars appeared in profusion, scattered across the heavens. Far from the ambient light of the city, millions of celestial bodies winked in the deep black sky.

In the distance, Sydney caught sight of the glow of a campfire. They were approaching a Bedouin village.

The laconic leader finally spoke. "Abaas Abdullah is expecting you. The evening meal will be prepared."

As they drew nearer the campfire, a young man walked out to meet them.

The group stopped, and the man addressed himself to Dixon, the senior visitor. "Greetings from my father, Abaas Abdullah. He bids you welcome to his camp and offers the hospitality of his table and his tent."

Dixon dismounted and replied in the same formal manner before following the young man into the village.

When Sydney and the others had arrived, they all joined the men for their evening meal.

Sydney listened as the men talked. She kept her head down, speaking only when she was spoken to. Abdullah asked Dixon polite questions but never raised the subject of business. It would be the height of bad manners to talk business over their meal.

The rest of the men drifted away slowly until

only Dixon, Sydney, and Abdullah remained. Abdullah offered them coffee and took the two of them on a tour of his small village.

"Since you came seeking me," Abdullah said, "I am sure you have business you wish to discuss. Would you care to tell me why you are here?"

"I believe you have something I am looking for." Dixon chose his words carefully. "Something that was entrusted to you by a man who died before he could reclaim it."

Sydney tensed, listening for any sound, any clue they were being watched or followed. She was Dixon's eyes and ears as he conducted the delicate negotiations.

Dixon continued talking, finally describing to Abdullah the locked chest Charlene had told them about. "It belonged to Abdul Kamal. I am told he was a business associate of yours before his death. I hoped you might be persuaded to part with it—for the right price."

"It must be valuable, for you to travel all the way out here to find it after all these years."

"I don't know," Dixon said. It was the truth. Charlene had told them about what Kamal had called his "insurance policy"—a stash of file copies that he had claimed would buy both their freedom and a comfortable retirement.

But she didn't know what the files contained.

Dixon, Sydney, the rest of the team—none of them knew if the chest would help or if it would be another dead end. But it was their only link to Kamal, and through him, to Jing.

"Phoenix." Jack Bristow's voice came over her comm from his backup position near Tamad. "This is Raptor. Your package has arrived."

One less worry. Charlene had arrived safely in Los Angeles and was in APO custody.

"Roger," Sydney whispered, her voice covered by the soft sighing of the night wind across the desert.

Dixon and Abdullah were deep in conversation about the chest. It was in Abdullah's possession. He didn't deny it. But he wasn't anxious to part with it.

"Name your price if you don't like my offer," Dixon said. "You have had the box for many years, yet you say it is still sealed. How much could it be worth to you?"

Abdullah drew himself up, indignation oozing from every pore. "Do you think I can put a price on trust? Kamal trusted me with his greatest treasure, so valuable even he could not guess its worth. He asked me to guard it with my life, and I have. Why would I give it to you?"

"Because you are a wise man," Dixon replied. "You know the value of trust and the value of objects. You have guarded Kamal's treasure well past the end of his life. His trust was well placed. But now it is only an object, nothing more."

As they turned a corner, Sydney caught a shadow moving at the edge of her vision. She didn't turn her head but cast her eyes to the side.

There it was again. Someone was stalking them, moving parallel with them, on the other side of the tents.

She slowed, dropping back a step. "Outrigger," she whispered over the comm, "we have company."

Dixon turned slightly, as though checking on his young companion. He caught her eye, acknowledging he had heard.

Sydney followed the two men along a line of tents, watching for the telltale movement of the person shadowing them.

When they reached Abdullah's tent, he invited them to come inside and sit for a while. He was not through bargaining with Dixon. In fact, he seemed to be enjoying the process.

Sydney sat to the side as the two men continued haggling. She peered around the spacious tent, looking for Kamal's chest. Charlene had described it as leather, with brass fittings and an ornate padlock.

She spotted what she thought was the chest, shoved under a low table to one side of the tent. A faint ripple in the fabric, a rustle caused by movement just outside, confirmed it. Someone was standing next to the chest on the other side of the tent wall. She coughed, a signal to Dixon that she had identified their target. Now all they had to do was convince Abdullah to part with the desired object.

But the tribal leader was proving to be extremely stubborn. Nothing Dixon offered enticed him, and even Dixon's remarkable calm was showing signs of wear.

As the two men continued, Sydney was aware of more movement outside the tent. She had counted the number of men in Abudllah's inner circle earlier: the three who had met them, Abdullah, his son Barak, and two others, brothers to their escorts.

Seven in all, against the two of them.

She couldn't deny the odds, but she was prepared to even them as quickly as possible if she had to.

Abdullah's voice rose. He was no longer enjoying the haggling with Dixon. His face reddened.

"Perhaps I do not even have the object you're looking for," he said. There was anger in his voice, challenging Dixon to argue with him.

"Perhaps not. But I don't think that is likely. Kamal told you the chest was valuable. You wouldn't get rid of it."

"If I tell you I do not have it . . . ?" Abdullah left the question hanging in the air.

"I will not believe you," Dixon replied. He was holding his ground, sparring with the old man.

"Then there is nothing more to discuss."

"But I think there is," Dixon persisted.

"And I think it is time for you to leave." Abdullah clapped his hands. His son appeared at the door with two of their escorts from earlier in the day. Each of the men wore a sword tucked in his sash, and the two escorts had their hands on the hilts. Barak stood with his arms crossed.

Dixon rose from his seat on the floor. He

straightened to his full height, from which he towered over the three men.

Sydney slid toward Abdullah, moving slowly. The three men were focused on Dixon. She had made herself nearly invisible all night, and no one noticed her now.

As she got close, she flipped open the scarab on a large ring on her right hand, uncovering a short needle, and twisted the ring around her finger.

While the men were still distracted, she reached out to Abdullah, grabbing his exposed hand. The needle bit into the soft tissue on the inside of his wrist, delivering an instant dose of a powerful tranquilizer.

Barak looked at his father as the older man slumped against Sydney. Seeing his father fall, he shouted, and lunged for her.

Sydney pushed away from the weight of the unconscious Abdullah and flipped the scarab closed, quickly twisting out of Barak's grasp.

Dixon had seen Barak lunge for Sydney. His two guards tensed, but Dixon blocked their path, preventing them from going to Barak's aid.

The two guards drew their swords. Dixon

backed up a step, keeping himself between the guards and Sydney and Barak. He drew his own sword.

He knew Barak's shout, coupled with the clash of swords, would draw the rest of the village to the tent. Dixon didn't need reinforcements arriving.

He shifted his sword to his left hand and pulled one of the ceremonial sashes from his waist. Hidden within the flowing silk was a strong, highly flexible chain.

Barak spun around to confront Sydney. She snapped her arm back, dislodging Barak's turban, which slipped over one eye.

Instinctively, Barak reached up to right the turban.

Sydney yanked a loose end of the coiled head-piece. Several yards of fabric unwound. Using the turban, Sydney moved in, whipping the fabric around Barak's raised wrists.

Dixon looped his sash around the blade of the guard on his right. The guard on the left lunged forward, his sword flashing. Dixon sidestepped the slashing blade and quickly threw two more loops over the sword of the guard on the right. He whipped the sash, twisting the blade in the guard's hand and breaking his grip. The sword fell, and the guard dove after it. Dixon lashed out with his right foot, catching him on the chin. The guard fell and didn't move.

Barak tried to pull his hands free of the turban wound around his wrists. He couldn't dislodge the restraints. He shifted his weight, creating some slack in the fabric. Before Sydney could take up the slack, Barak jerked hard, pulling her off balance.

Sydney relaxed into the motion, letting Barak's force pull her toward him. She lowered her head and sprang at him, butting into his midsection.

She heard a muffled *ooof* as Barak absorbed the impact. She drove forward, adding the power of her own lunge to Barak's pull. The combined momentum folded Barak in two and sent him to the floor.

Dixon extricated his sash from the sword of the unconscious guard. He turned to confront the other guard, whose sword was poised for another slash. The body of his comrade was between them.

The guard lunged over his fallen man, but Dixon moved out of the way. He caught the man with the flat of his sword against the side of his head.

The guard's head rocked, and he stumbled. Dixon threw his sash around the guard's neck and pulled it tight.

Sydney landed on top of Barak, pinning him to the floor. He was stronger than he looked and managed to throw her off, but he looked puzzled.

Though he seemed poised to attack, he hesitated. There was something odd about his assailant.

Sydney didn't give him time to think about it.

She leaped onto his back, throwing him face-first into the floor. She flipped the scarab open and plunged the needle into his neck. The ring contained only two doses, but she still closed it carefully. Marshall was always pleased when they returned his special toys.

Dixon twisted the sash around the neck of the remaining guard, cutting off his air supply. The man thrashed, trying to throw Dixon off, but his movements were weak and uncoordinated, and he slowly subsided, sinking to the floor.

Sydney and Dixon moved from one man to the next, tying them securely with sashes and turbans. Barak and Abdullah would be asleep for at least eight hours, but they weren't taking any chances.

Sydney dashed to the side of the tent and grabbed the chest from under the small table. She tucked it under her arm and joined Dixon at the entrance.

Dixon took a wad of American bills from inside his robe and placed them in Abdullah's lap. They equaled his last offer, with a generous bonus. It might soften Abdullah's anger when he woke up.

There had been little noise after Barak's initial shout. No one had come to investigate, and Sydney's hopes rose when they listened at the door of the tent and heard nothing.

But they still had to reach the fenced area where the camels were kept. They would have to find their mounts, saddle them, and escape without alerting the entire village.

They were far from safe.

The two agents crept through the tent door, crouched low, their breath shallow. They moved carefully along the side of the tent and cautiously peered around the corner into the darkness.

Nothing moved, and after several seconds Dixon signaled Sydney to follow him as he slipped around the corner.

Ahead, they heard the soft lowing of the camels

and the shuffling of the animals in their corral.

As they drew nearer, they saw two men walking away, and heard them talking about finding coffee.

Sydney and Dixon crept into the camel paddock. The saddles and tack were hung over one of the fence rails. Sydney set the chest on the ground and looked for their saddles.

Dixon moved cautiously among the animals, searching for their mounts. Camels were symbols of wealth and status among the Bedouins. Taking the wrong animal would be far worse than anything they had done so far.

He spotted their camels, signaling to Sydney to bring the saddles. Between them, they hoisted a saddle onto each camel's back and adjusted the girth.

Dixon lashed the chest to the back of one saddle, securing it for their journey.

They were nearly ready to go. Dixon led the camels to the gate and ordered them to *cush*, or kneel, so they could mount. Sydney lowered the gnarled tree limb that formed the gate of the enclosure.

Just then the two men returned, accompanied by a third guard. All three carried brass cups of steaming coffee. Their conversation stopped suddenly as they spotted the two visitors standing at the entrance to the enclosure with their camels.

The three men did not wait for their comrades. They charged Sydney and Dixon, brandishing their swords and yelling for the rest of the men to join them.

Dixon drew his sword, no longer concerned about the noise. He caught the blade of one of the charging men and deflected the blow. The clash of steel on steel rang through the village.

Sydney slid between the other two men as they ran at her. She pirouetted and slipped a pair of small daggers from her sash. She preferred the shorter stabbing weapons to the slashing swords the others carried.

She leaped after the men, landing a flying kick on the back of one. He went down, spread-eagled on the hard ground. His sword skittered away, and he scrambled after it. The second man whirled on Sydney, his sword swinging in a broad arc toward her.

Dixon deflected another blow from his attacker. The blades slid against each other as Dixon turned away, his robes swirling around him.

Sydney narrowly avoided her assailant's flashing blade. Sliding backward, she nearly tripped over the slumbering form of a camel.

Trapped between the camel and the guard, she lifted her robes out of the way and leaped atop the sleeping animal. The camel started and climbed to its feet as Sydney jumped off on the other side, putting the camel between her and the attacker.

She heard the startled cry of her pursuer as he tried to avoid hitting the camel with his sword, and the slap as the flat òf the blade smacked against the beast.

The camel bleated his displeasure and swung his head toward his assailant. The guard jumped back, narrowly avoiding the teeth of the angry camel.

Dixon spun around, facing his attacker. He ran at the man, his sword held steady. When he was within a few feet, he swung the blade. He felt the sudden jolt of contact, then resistance. The blade stopped for a moment, then continued its arc as it sliced into the guard's thigh. The man fell, screaming in pain.

Women and children were emerging from the tents, startled by the screams and the noise of clashing swords.

A couple of older boys ventured close. Dixon

worried they might consider joining the fight. He didn't want to hurt a kid.

Sydney appeared at Dixon's side.

"Let's go!" she shouted.

Dixon leaped into his saddle, and Sydney did the same. They urged the camels to their feet. The camels rose and pushed through the gathering villagers.

Sydney risked a look over her shoulder. One of the guards had managed to maneuver past the angry camel. Sword upraised, he ran toward Sydney and Dixon.

Sydney still had a dagger in her hand. It was hard to gauge distance in the dark, but she aimed as best she could from the back of a rocking camel and threw the knife at their pursuer.

She heard a scream. The knife had found its target.

She turned back to the desert in front of them, an eerie, empty landscape in the pale moonlight, and urged her camel into a trot.

They rode fast for ten minutes, then slowed to rest the animals. Dixon strained his ears for the sounds of pursuit, but he didn't hear anything.

They sped up again, running for another five minutes.

As they slowed, Sydney checked her GPS. "Raptor," she spoke over the comm, "this is Phoenix. We have the package."

"Roger, Phoenix. Are you clear of the village?"

"We're three or four miles away. Are you ready for extraction?"

"On our way, Phoenix. We'll be waiting for you."

"Good." Sydney wiggled in her saddle, pulling her arms inside her robes and tugging at her body-suit. "The sooner I can get out of this mummy wrap, the better."

On the other end of the comm, she heard her father chuckle.

CHAPTER 18

APO HEADQUARTERS
LOS ANGELES, CALIFORNIA

Arvin Sloane stood over Sydney's desk, his hand resting on the back of her chair. She sat completely still, resisting the urge to shove his hand away.

"That was good work in Sinai, Sydney."

She didn't answer until she was sure she could control her voice. "Thank you, sir. Just doing my job."

"You do it well, Sydney. I'm very proud of you."

There was nothing she could say. Sloane insisted that he thought of her as a daughter, in spite of everything that had passed between them, in spite of the existence of his own daughter, her half sister.

For Nadia's sake, if not her own, she held her tongue.

Sloane moved off, heading back to his office, and Sydney released the breath she didn't know she had been holding.

"Steady."

She looked up and caught Dixon smiling at her from a few feet away. She smiled back. Dixon had his own issues with Sloane, but he managed to keep his cool. It was a quality she admired, even when she couldn't emulate it.

"You did do a good job, you know," Dixon continued, moving closer to her desk. "That box is keeping Sloane and your father very busy."

She glanced into Sloane's office, where her father and her boss were bent over the papers that were spread across the glass top of Sloane's normally pristine desk.

"Have they said anything to you about what's in there?" she asked, turning back to Dixon.

"Not yet." Dixon shook his head. "It was so late when we got back, I just headed home to see the kids. Got there in time for dinner, then they had to go to bed. But at least I was there for breakfast this morning." He shook off the wave of melancholy that passed over him. His home life suffered sometimes, but he worked hard at maintaining a connection with his children. "I haven't had time to talk with Jack or Sloane since. They've been in there all night, according to Marshall, so there must be something worthwhile in those files."

"I did talk to my dad for a few minutes," Sydney said. "He said there were lists of Kamal's contacts. He was working with Jing, and there are names of all the people within the Alliance that were working with them."

Dixon's eyes widened. "We hit the jackpot, then?"

"Sounds like it. There were also bank account records. They put Marshall on those, hacking the bank databases, to see if they can find recent activity." They had hit the jackpot indeed.

A couple of hours later, as Sydney was finishing her formal report on the Sinai operation, she was called into Sloane's office, along with Dixon.

Sloane sat at his desk, the top now cleared of clutter. A single file folder remained.

"This"—Sloane tapped the file folder with an outstretched finger—"was invaluable. There were names and dates and financial information. We'll go over it with the team in a few minutes"—he glanced at his watch—"but I wanted to congratulate you two personally. Your work—getting Charlene Davies to cooperate and retrieving this box—may have been the break we needed."

"Thank you," Sydney said stiffly. She didn't want Sloane singling her out for anything, and she didn't care about his praise. Pleasing Arvin Sloane meant nothing to her.

"Well." Sloane rose from his chair and extended his hand across the desk. "Thank you both."

Dixon shook Sloane's hand, but Sydney slipped out of her chair and reached the door without any further contact.

"You have to talk to him sometimes," Dixon said, coming up next to her outside Sloane's office.

"Only when I can't avoid it," Sydney shot back. She turned away from Dixon and went back to her report.

A few minutes later, as promised, Sloane called the team into the conference room, saying there was information regarding the mission.

"Ladies and gentlemen," Sloane said as soon as they were all assembled, "we have learned a great deal in the last few hours. Thanks to the information retrieved from the Sinai"—he looked quickly at Dixon and Sydney, acknowledging their contribution—"we now have a list of Mr. Kamal's associates. One of them was Gai Dong Jing, and it is clear the two of them were working together. Jack?"

Jack Bristow rose from his seat and stood straight, his hands clasped behind his back. His suit was neatly pressed, his white shirt crisp, and his tie perfectly knotted.

Sydney knew he had worked all night, yet he managed to look immaculately groomed, as though he had just arrived. It was just another manifestation of her father's iron will.

"Mr. Kamal and his associate Mr. Jing were worried about two things: that the Alliance would succeed, and that it wouldn't. Either way, their value to the organization was, they believed, doomed to shrink.

"With that in mind, they set out to insure themselves against both possibilities. They recruited like-minded individuals and established a shadow organization within the Alliance. Their goal was to insulate themselves from either outcome. If the Alliance succeeded, they planned to have enough intelligence secreted to insure their own immunity, and enough money to buy a long and pleasurable retirement. If the Alliance failed, they planned to simply walk away with whatever assets they could take."

Jack paused and consulted the notes on the table in front of him. Although he had already memorized the details, he still double-checked them before continuing.

"They assembled a team: disgruntled agents— pragmatists, not idealists. People who were available for a price. They began siphoning money. The box Sydney and Dixon retrieved contained records of all of it. We have spent the past several hours checking on every name on that list. Some were in custody, but most of them died in the raids, like Kamal. We knew Kamal was dead, killed by the Shin Bet. The only one unaccounted for was Jing, and now we know why. We have the recent video evidence." He clicked a remote and the monitors sprang to life with video from the Vladivostok police station. "Gai Dong Jing is alive and well. Whatever assets remain are under his control. And he is trying to reassemble his team."

Sloane nodded at Jack and resumed his spot at the front of the room. "Since Jing has Dr. Alexyeev, and we have the doctor's research, it seems clear that Jing is trying to revive the bioweapons program. It is also clear that Dr. Alexyeev may know more about the program than we initially thought. As of this moment, our primary objective must be the retrieval of Dr. Alexyeev. He must be freed from Jing's captivity and brought here so that we can find out what he knows."

Sloane paused dramatically.

"I want Alexyeev."

Sydney stared at the table, unable to look at Sloane. If Alexyeev did have information about a bioweapon, she couldn't imagine letting that kind of power fall into the hands of Arvin Sloane. She knew what Sloane was capable of, and a powerful biological weapon was not something she was willing to trust him with.

"Mr. Flinkman, do you have something to add?"

"Sure." Marshall flipped through his notes. "We have traced at least three bank accounts, thanks to the stuff Sydney and Dixon brought back." He looked over at Sydney. "By the way, did you really ride camels? I was curious, and, well—" He caught a look from Sloane and quickly put an end to his tangent. "Could I talk to you later?"

"Of course." Sydney smiled at him.

"As for the banks," Marshall continued, "we've found several million dollars, most of it in accounts that are *almost* dormant. They have just enough activity to keep them active, but nothing more. I'm working on tracking other accounts, but it will take time."

"Time, Mr. Flinkman," Sloane broke in, "is something we do not have. As Agent Weiss told us, this virus is mutating and has the potential for immeasurable damage."

Marshall bobbed his head. "Certainly, Mr. Sloane. I just meant, well, that I'll keep working on it, as fast as I can."

"Which, I hope," Sloane replied flatly, "will be enough."

"We do have one other thing," Marshall said. His voice was uncharacteristically subdued, and his expression somber. He clicked the remote, changing the display from the police station video still to the photo of a young boy.

"This is the picture of one of the suspected virus victims." Marshall's voice was thick, and he swallowed hard. "He was just a little boy, in Hong Kong."

Sydney's startled cry drew all eyes to her stricken face. "That's the boy from the pictures in the bunker," she said. "I'm sure of it."

Marshall bobbed his head in agreement. "I ran an analysis of this photograph against the ones from the bunker. It's the same child."

A copy of the boy's death certificate was passed to each of the agents. Sydney dug through her notes, looking for the information on the bunker photos, the dates of the photographs.

When she found them, her heart squeezed in sympathy. The last picture, where the woman looked so sad and worn out, was only a couple of weeks after the boy's death. What Sydney saw in the picture was grief, draining the life and the beauty from a mother who had just lost her child.

Sydney stared at the copies of the pictures from the bunker. "They look like a family," she murmured. "But where are they now? Where is the boy's mother? And why was Alexyeev alone in that laboratory?"

She looked up, avoiding Sloane and her father. Instead she addressed Marshall. "Do we know anything more about them?"

"Not yet," Marshall said softly, clearly thinking of his own little boy. The death of this child had obviously affected him. "But we will."

"Sydney." Arvin Sloane stopped her before she could leave the conference room. "A word."

Sydney waited. Sloane also stopped Nadia, and he motioned for the two women to follow him to his office.

"I have a mission for the two of you," he said. "I'm sending you to Hong Kong. That's where the boy died, and I want you to find his mother. She may be able to lead us to Alexyeev. As sexist as it may sound," he said with a little smile, "I am hoping the two of you will be able to appeal to the woman in a more personal way."

Sydney bit back a retort. Much as she hated Sloane's implication, he could be right, which only made it worse.

"There is a plane waiting," Sloane continued. "You can leave within the hour. I know I can count on you two."

Sloane smiled warmly, sending chills down Sydney's back.

CHAPTER 19

THE FLOATING CITY
ABERDEEN HARBOUR, HONG KONG, CHINA

Sydney sat in the rear of the tiny sampan, navigating slowly between the larger boats. By the time she and Nadia had landed in Hong Kong, Marshall had provided them with the last known address of the boy's mother. She had lived aboard a boat in Aberdeen Harbour, in the area known as the Floating City.

Sydney marveled at the scene around her—boats of all sizes and shapes packed into floating neighborhoods. Some were lashed together, others floated free, but all of them were crowded with people. Extended families, from babies to aging grandparents, lined the rails or sat on the decks.

It was a far cry from the isolated bunker in the forest of North Korea. There, Alexyeev had no neighbors, and even the people of the nearby village avoided the area, if the men she'd heard were right.

Here, everything teemed with people, many millions of them. The streets were always full, and the harbor pulsed with activity day and night.

It was hard to reconcile the image of Alexyeev, alone in his bunker, with the bustling city where the mother of his children lived. It was hard to imagine a more unlikely combination, yet the couple had produced a son, and apparently two daughters, judging by the photographs.

They slid between a pair of boats. Tires hung on the sides of the larger vessels provided a barrier to collisions. As they passed the boats, Sydney spotted a pleasant-looking young woman on board one of them.

Sydney reversed the outboard motor that powered the sampan and it drifted alongside the bigger boat. She called to the woman on deck.

"I'm looking for a woman," she said.

"It looks like you already have one." The woman on the boat waved a hand at Nadia. "What do you want with another one?"

Sydney grinned and stood up carefully. She held out a copy of a bunker photograph, one where Alexyeev's wife was smiling. "I'm looking for this woman," she said. "Do you know her or where I might find someone who does?"

The woman took the photograph and held it at arm's length, turning it from side to side. "She looks familiar," she said at last. "I think she used to live over there." She gestured to a cluster of boats a short distance away. "Talk to Mei Mei; she knew her."

The woman handed the picture back, and Sydney thanked her.

She and Nadia spent the next two hours going from one cluster of boats to another. Mei Mei no longer lived where the woman had told them, but someone there pointed to another area of the Floating City.

It was getting dark and the lights of Hong Kong were coming on when they approached yet another cluster of boats.

Syd fought off a sense of futility and a rising

uneasiness. If they didn't find something here, they would have to come back in the morning. Even for her and Nadia, this wasn't a place to wander around in the dark.

When they asked for Mei Mei at the next dock, a young boy spoke up. "That's my mother," he said, and raced off to summon her, leaping fearlessly between boats and dodging under clotheslines.

Sydney waited as the night grew darker and the points of light that dotted the city merged into a solid glow. Lighted windows and displays of neon covered the city, and on the water the ferries glowed brightly. Even the Floating City itself was lit up, with lanterns and cookstoves creating an eerie flickering illumination. Sydney wondered if she should trust the child to return and whether his mother would actually accompany him.

When he finally came back, he was alone. "My mother says to come to our boat," he told her. "Just follow me."

It was easier said than done. He took off as before, moving through the tangle of boats, as Sydney maneuvered her sampan, trying to keep him in sight.

He stopped when he reached a large boat with a smaller boat tied alongside. The smaller boat was covered with nets, and fish hung from racks on the deck of the larger boat.

At the side, waiting for the boy, was a woman in her thirties, holding a toddler. She placed her arm protectively around the boy when he came onto the boat.

"Are you Mei Mei?" Sydney asked as they drew alongside.

"Why do you ask?"

"I was told to talk to you, that you might know the woman in this picture." Sydney held out the photo as she had done all afternoon. The corners were bent, and there was a large crease across the top, the result of repeated handling.

The woman stared silently at the picture, her emotions clear in her face. She knew the woman, but there was an underlying sadness in her look of recognition.

Nadia spoke softly, not moving from her seat at the front of the sampan. "You know her, don't you, Mei Mei?"

The woman nodded, but she still didn't speak.

"Do you know where she is?" Nadia continued,

rising slowly to her feet. "Do you know where we can find her?"

"She's gone," Mei Mei said. Her voice cracked, and she sounded hoarse.

"Gone?" Sydney said. "Gone where?"

Mei Mei waved an arm toward the hillside in the distance.

"Is she in the city?" Nadia asked.

"No." The woman shook her head. "The authorities would not allow us to bury her. Only her ashes remain."

Sydney's heart sank. They had followed this faint trail across the globe, only to have it fade out in the dark night of Aberdeen Harbour.

"I'm so sorry," Nadia said quickly. "She was your friend, and I'm sorry she's gone."

"Can you tell us about her?" Sydney asked. She didn't dare hope, but she couldn't let it stop her from trying. "We need to know."

The woman shrugged.

Beside her, the little boy fidgeted away from her encircling arm, anxious to be on the move. Sydney, seeing his impatience, reached in the small pack slung around her waist. She pulled out a wad of Hong Kong dollars and held them out to him. "For helping us find your mom," she said.

The boy's eyes widened. It was likely the most money that he had ever seen at one time in his short life.

He glanced up at his mother before taking it, Sydney noted with satisfaction. His mother nodded, and he snatched the notes from her hand.

"Thanks, lady!" The notes disappeared into his shirt, though Sydney suspected they would find their way into his mother's pocket soon enough. But the fiction was maintained that they were merely thanking the boy for his help.

"She is beyond harm now," Mei Mei said. "Come aboard. I will make tea, and we can talk about my friend, Ming."

Nadia climbed up onto the boat, and Sydney followed, securing the sampan to the larger boat until their return trip to the mainland.

Mei Mei brewed tea and served her guests. As she did, she told the two sisters about Ming.

"She lived near me, before Rong was born." Mei Mei motioned toward the toddler, who sat a few feet away. Across the back and sides of the deck, netting was strung to prevent his falling overboard. Sydney realized she had seen similar arrangements several times that afternoon. Now she understood why.

"Was she married then?" Nadia asked.

"If you could call it that." There was a note of disgust in Mei Mei's reply. "She married that Russian doctor, the one she met at the university."

"She was a student at the university?"

"No. She worked there. She cleaned in the chemistry section. The doctor came here to teach, and she fell, hard. Before you knew it, they were married."

"It doesn't sound as if you liked him," Sydney said evenly.

Mei Mei held her head to one side for a moment, thinking. "I guess he was okay. But he didn't treat her very well. Right after they were married, he left the university, told her he had this great job, but he had to go away all the time. Left her here, alone, for weeks at a time. Of course, she wasn't alone long. Uri was born that first year. He was a sweet baby, and she was very happy. But his father wasn't even here when he was born."

Sydney and Nadia murmured sympathetically. Nadia's father hadn't been there when she was born, and Jack Bristow had been absent most of

Sydney's life. They both understood what it meant for Ming to be alone, isolated.

Syd felt anger rise up. It may have been Alexyeev's job that kept him away, but that really meant the Alliance. The organization that had haunted so many of her adult years was responsible for the destruction of yet another family.

Nadia took copies of all the bunker pictures from her purse and handed them to Mei Mei. "This is her husband, right? And I'm guessing the little boy is Uri. But what about the infants? These pictures were taken at different times, yet there is a baby in each of them."

Mei Mei's eyes instantly swam with tears. "She had three children," she said in a choked voice. "First Uri, then two little girls. He"—she spat the word—"wasn't here, of course."

She swallowed hard and regained her composure. "He came home a couple of weeks after the first daughter was born. Soon after, she got very sick. She went into convulsions and died. It was horrible! If it hadn't been for Uri, I think Ming would have died of a broken heart. Soon she was pregnant again, though, with the baby girl in that second photo, there," she said, pointing. "She was only a few days old when they took that picture. Ming really thought things would be better, now that she had another daughter. But this baby didn't even live as long as the first one. She got a fever and developed sores all over her body. It was a horrible thing to see. And Ming had already been through it once. The second time was even worse."

Nadia shuddered. She had seen the pictures of Kono from the Vladivostok morgue. It *was* horrible, especially since these had been infants, so small and fragile, dependent on the adults around them to keep them safe.

Sydney set her teacup on the table. "Did the doctors find out what killed them?"

Mei Mei shook her head. "We are poor people. No one cared enough to investigate."

"But the boy," Nadia said. "He didn't get sick?"

"Not at first, like the girls. But eventually he did. He died the same way."

Nadia and Sydney exchanged a long look. They dealt in death and disaster every day, but this touched them deeply.

"Anyway, that was the beginning of the end for Ming. Her husband was gone, again, and she became despondent. She was convinced it was her fault her children had died, and nothing I could say or do would make a difference. I thought she would get over it, but it just got worse. And then one day"—she made a slicing motion across her wrist—"she was gone. I never saw her husband after that. He didn't even come back for her funeral," she said bitterly.

It had grown late as the women talked. Sydney and Nadia thanked Mei Mei for her help and climbed back into their sampan. As they moved away, across the dark water, they watched Mei Mei silhouetted in the light from her boat, the toddler Rong once again riding her hip, and the boy standing close by her side.

Another sampan stopped next to the boat, and a slender man climbed aboard. He greeted Mei Mei with a kiss and lifted the baby in his arms. It was a heartwarming tableau. But it couldn't erase the horror Sydney and Nadia had heard about from Mei Mei only moments earlier.

Sydney and Nadia boarded the jet to Los Angeles immediately after their visit to the Floating City. Both sisters were exhausted by what they had seen and heard, but neither one could sleep.

They sat facing each other, the cabin lights turned low. Soft music, an unexceptional jazz composition, played in the background. The seats were comfortable, cushioning the weary travelers.

But instead of relaxing, they each stared out the window into the blackness of night over the empty ocean.

The silence stretched between them until Sydney couldn't stand it any longer.

"That was horrible," she said.

Her voice was soft, so soft Nadia could have pretended not to hear her. She didn't.

"One of the worst things I have ever had to listen to," she replied. "Those babies, and that poor woman! For her to think that she caused it. How sad."

Sydney stared out the window. Her usual anger when she thought of the Alliance was replaced by a terrible sadness. The Alliance had kept Alexyeev from his children and had finally sent him back to them, carrying the poison that killed them. "She never knew why they died—never knew it wasn't her fault, that the Alliance took her husband and her children."

Nadia reached over and turned her sister's face

to look at her. "Are you thinking only of her, Sydney?"

Sydney tried to avoid her sister's gaze, to not hear the quaver in her voice, but she couldn't. Her eyes locked with her sister's, and she saw the tears threatening to spill over.

"No," Sydney answered, her own voice unsteady. "I wasn't."

She stopped, but Nadia was patient. She could wait for Sydney as long as necessary.

"I was thinking of me, too. And you. How it was to grow up without a father, like Uri."

Nadia sat back. "I don't know which is worse," she said. "I never knew my father, but you knew yours, and then you lost him when our mother died."

Sydney shook her head. "I don't know either."

CHAPTER 20

APO HEADQUARTERS
LOS ANGELES, CALIFORNIA

Sydney and Nadia made their way through the security system and into APO headquarters. They had talked for hours as they crossed the Pacific, not stopping until they reached the house they shared and fell into bed, exhausted.

For Sydney, having a sister was still new and exciting. She had grown up as an only child, and finding Nadia had been like a gift. She was learning to treasure the connection they had forged. The trip to Hong Kong had made her even more aware of how much her sister already meant to her.

253

While the sisters were traveling, the rest of the team had followed up on the information they had received from Mei Mei. Alexyeev had supposedly left the Korean bioweapons program when it was shut down, but Mei Mei said he had been gone for long stretches.

Had he been hiding in the bunker beneath the BiMedTech facility all that time?

And where was he now?

Vaughn and Jack had reached out to their allies around the globe. Sloane mined his contacts in the shadowy world of international crime. Weiss, Dixon, and Marshall combed through terabytes of data. But aside from the Friday Market sighting, no one had seen Jing since the raid on the police station in Vladivostok.

Well, one person had seen Alexyeev since the raid—Kai-Jin Kono, and she was dead. How long before there was another death?

Sydney found herself thinking about Alexyeev as she wrote her report. He was out there, some-where, alone. His wife and children were dead, his work destroyed.

He was completely isolated.

Sloane made a slow circuit of the office, checking the progress of each member of the team. As he bent over Nadia's desk, Sydney wondered again about what her sister had said. Was it worse not to ever know your father, or to lose him?

When Sloane approached Sydney's desk, she stiffened. He might be Nadia's father, but she still could not forgive the things he had done.

"Have you found any sign of Jing?" she asked him.

Sloane sighed. "None, I'm afraid. We're tapping every source of intel, but he seems to have disappeared. Finding Alexyeev is our primary objective now. He is the key to everything. We need the knowledge that's locked in his brain, the things that aren't in the journals."

"How are we doing with those?"

"Jack is doing the translations, but they're also coded. It's a slow process."

Sydney turned back to her report. "I'll have this for you soon," she said, "although I doubt there is much here that's useful."

"Thank you." Sloane hesitated, but Sydney kept her attention resolutely on the screen in front of her, and he turned away.

* * *

This was the part Sydney hated. Waiting.

She looked around the office. The team had been working around the clock, checking and rechecking their intel, cajoling information from their contacts.

Suddenly, Marshall whooped with joy.

It took Sydney a few seconds to process the interruption. When she realized where it had come from, she jumped to her feet and joined the rest of the team converging on the cluttered lab.

"Got him!" Marshall crowed as the agents crowded into his workspace. "Right there!" He pointed to a bank surveillance video displayed on his monitor.

Sloane pushed to the front of the small crowd and peered over Marshall's shoulder. On the monitor in front of him was a freeze-frame of Gai Dong Jing. He was standing at a teller window with a check in his hand.

"The bank tapes every transaction," Marshall said. "Once I had a time and place, courtesy of the account records, all I had to do was hack the video system and find the file with this picture."

Marshall tapped his keyboard, zooming in on Jing's hand holding the check. The tattoo on his wrist filled the screen.

"It's him," Jack said from his spot at the rear of the group. "Where is this from, Marshall?"

"Tokyo," Marshall replied. "Bank of Tokyo, near the Ginza."

"All right." Sloane took command of the impromptu meeting. "Everyone, now that Marshall has narrowed our search, I want all of you to concentrate on your Japanese assets."

He turned to Dixon. "You will lead the team. I want you, Sydney, Nadia, and Weiss on your way within the hour. Jack will direct operations here, with help from Vaughn. Marshall, you will continue with the decryption of the bunker notes. If Alexyeev is in Tokyo, I want everything we have on him before anyone gets near him. Okay, people. We finally have a solid lead. Let's make the most of it. We need Peotr Alexyeev—now."

The team scattered. They each had an assignment, and they had the excitement that the sighting provided. The energy in the office was palpable as the agents moved with renewed purpose.

Sydney joined Nadia, Weiss, and Dixon in the conference room as Dixon hastily sketched their plan, which was basically to fly to Tokyo and proceed with whatever information the rest of the team could assemble while they were in the air.

"We'll just play this by ear," Dixon said. "Improvisation will be the key on this mission."

"What about op tech?" Weiss asked.

"Take whatever you think you might need," Dixon replied. "We have no idea what we're walking into, but there is a safe house in Tokyo that we can use for a base of operations." Dixon glanced around the table. "Are you ready?"

He was met with a murmur of assent.

"Then let's go."

The four agents left the conference room and grabbed their hastily assembled gear. Within minutes they were on their way to the waiting jet.

Sydney and Nadia had been home less than eight hours.

CHAPTER 21

APO SAFE HOUSE
TOKYO, JAPAN

Inside the safe house, the APO team assembled, reviewing the latest intel from Los Angeles.

It was easy, according to Marshall, to follow Jing's trail of bank activity. Although his transactions were funneled through a series of accounts, and the trail was convoluted, Marshall had traced each movement and transaction as Jing moved around Tokyo. With that information and security video from around the city, Marshall had identified some of Jing's favorite places.

Dixon detailed the mission plan. "We have

three locations right now, and Marshall says he is working on at least one more. Sydney, you and I will be going to look at an apartment. Marshall has video showing Jing has made several visits to the building, but he isn't listed as a tenant. We will need to get access to their security logs to see what name he's using. We'll go by cab so the van won't be associated with our visit.

"Nadia, you and Weiss are going out later tonight. It seems the two of you are rich Americans, with a fat bank account and a taste for expensive nightlife. There is a nightclub downtown where Jing spends a lot of time and money. Sydney and I will be your backup."

Dixon looked at Sydney. "As soon as you're ready, we can go look at that apartment. Jack will let us know if there are any developments."

Sydney rose from her chair and headed for one of the two tiny bedrooms. "Ten minutes," she said.

While she changed, Dixon went over backup procedures with Nadia and Weiss, who would be on the comm link with him and Sydney. The bustling city, with its densely packed population, would be a challenge, but he was sure Marshall's op tech was more than equal to the task. He just hoped there was something worth reporting.

A few minutes later, Sydney emerged from the bedroom. She wore a scarlet linen dress with a thigh-high slit and a matching coat with a pinwheel hat. Her hair was pulled back in an elegant knot at the nape of her neck, and the extravagant stones in her earrings would fool all but the most expert diamond merchants.

"Darling," she said to Dixon, her voice finishing-school perfect. She held out her arm. "Shouldn't we be going?"

She threw Nadia a kiss, careful not to actually touch the carefully applied makeup that perfectly defined her mouth, and led the way out of the apartment.

On the street, Dixon hailed a cab, and they settled in for the trip to the apartment building. The midday traffic was not as bad as the morning rush hour had been, but the streets were still congested.

Dixon spoke quietly in English over the comm. "Evergreen, Houdini, do you read?"

Nadia answered. "Outrigger, this is Evergreen. Your signal is weak. Can you try the other band?"

Dixon tapped the tiny earpiece and tried again.

But after several minutes, there was no reply. He tapped again, moving back to the original frequency.

Nadia replied. "We heard nothing, Outrigger. I guess we better stay with this frequency."

"Roger," Dixon said. He glanced at Sydney, who had been watching the driver while Dixon was talking.

She shook her head briefly. The driver, like most Tokyo cabbies, didn't speak any English. Still, they kept their conversation low, inaudible against the background noise of the city that filled the streets around them, and they didn't speak of anything important.

The lobby of the high-rise was sleek and modern, the furnishings spare, elegant, and obviously expensive. As Dixon approached the desk, Sydney hung back. She sat on the edge of a sleek blond wood chair, fingering her designer sunglasses as though trying to decide whether to remove them or not.

In reality, she was using a scanner that Marshall had built into the lenses.

"See here?" he'd said. "This set of rhinestones? They're really directional controls. You touch one, the focus moves that way: left, right, up, down. Here, try it."

He'd put the glasses on her face, and Sydney had been momentarily disoriented by the sudden change in the world around her. She had wavered a little, and Marshall had sprung forward, grabbing the glasses.

"Forgot to warn you about that," he'd said, fiddling with the earpiece. "Here." He showed her a miniature slide switch. "That turns off the scanner, so they're just, you know, very cool sunglasses. Then you turn them on, and you have X-ray vision, like the ads in the back of the comic books, except these cost a lot more than two seventy-five and return postage. Oh, and they work, which the comic book ones didn't. I mean, not that I actually bought them or anything."

Now, prepared for the disorientation that came when walls and furniture became shadows and human beings turned into skeletons, she slid the switch.

The open lobby area took on a greenish glow, and she watched a group of skeletons walk past. When they had moved on, she could see Dixon, or skeleton Dixon, at the desk, talking with a skeleton clerk.

The clerk left Dixon alone at the desk and went into a back office. With the scanner working, Sydney could follow his movements as he approached someone and motioned them toward the front counter.

Sydney switched off the scanner for a moment and watched the desk. There were now two men talking to Dixon, one of whom was clearly a salesman. Dixon had his full attention as he withdrew a jet-black credit card from his wallet.

Over the comm link, Sydney heard the two men offer Dixon a tour of the building, including the rooftop garden, private spa, and members-only dining room.

Dixon seized on the idea of the dining room, as though pleasantly surprised by the amenity. "Ah, an excellent idea. You wouldn't mind joining me for a late lunch, would you? I just this minute realized how famished I am!"

The salesman agreed instantly, but told Dixon the clerk would have to remain on duty at the desk. Dixon's face clouded. "Not even a cup of tea?" he asked. "Or coffee?"

The displeasure in his voice, and his exclusive credit card, were enough to change the man's mind.

"Give us just a moment," he said, "to forward the incoming calls to the answering service."

The clerk ducked behind the desk and punched a series of codes into his telephone console. "All set," he said, coming back around. "Right this way, please."

Dixon followed the clerk, with the salesman close by his side. The man was already well into his pitch, extolling the virtues of the building, before they rounded a corner.

Sydney switched the scanner back on and watched the three men walk away.

She switched back off and took a fast look around the lobby. She was alone. She used the scanner to check the back office, where the salesman had been. It was still empty.

Sydney crossed the lobby, striding quickly in her towering heels, digging in her purse with one hand. To anyone entering the lobby, she appeared to be simply looking for her keys in the cavernous handbag she carried.

When she reached the office door, it was locked, as she had expected. But her picks, already in her hand, made short work of the barrier, and she slipped inside.

She slid her coat off and draped it on the coat

tree in the corner of the room, where the sales-man's suit coat had hung earlier.

"Outrigger, this is Phoenix. I'm in."

Dixon didn't reply, but she could hear him talk-ing with the clerk and salesman as they ordered their late lunch.

On one wall of the office, a bank of security monitors displayed black-and-white pictures from throughout the building. She could see Dixon on a monitor, with his back to the camera, and his two companions.

"Wonderful!" Dixon was saying to the sales-man. It was an acknowledgment they had agreed upon, one which fit his expansive alias.

The apartment's sales materials on the Web site had touted their security and discretion, prom-ising tenants absolute privacy in return for their large fees. But Marshall was more than equal to the challenge.

Sydney withdrew a thin sheet of rolled-up plastic from her bag. She shut off the computer's wireless keyboard and activated the membrane-thin code breaker.

"Evergreen, this is Phoenix."

"Roger, Phoenix."

"I'm in position," Sydney said.

Just then she heard footsteps in the hall. Grabbing the code breaker, she ducked behind the desk and waited.

The doorknob rattled, and she slipped her scanner sunglasses back on. Through the desk, she could see someone at the door. His fingers were clutched as though they were carrying something, but the scanner turned the object into nothing more than a faint green shadow.

The person knocked and waited, shifting from one foot to the other for a few seconds before walking away.

Sydney slid the switch on her glasses and pushed them up onto her head. "Sorry, Evergreen," she said. "Someone at the door. Gone now."

Sydney put the code breaker back in place and keyed the instruction sequence.

"Ready to transfer," she said:

"Ready to receive, Phoenix," Nadia replied from the safe house.

Sydney pushed a button, and lights glowed across the device as the computer's memory was scanned, compacted, and sent out as tiny bursts of seemingly random electronic noise.

While the transmission continued, Sydney made a rapid search of the paper files. She riffled through the desk drawers, finding nothing more interesting than letterhead in both English and Japanese versions, and a stash of Swiss chocolate in the bottom desk drawer.

She looked around the sparsely furnished room, clearly designed for efficiency, not comfort. There was probably another, more luxurious space for client meetings. The only decoration was a gaudy display of sales awards. Two file cabinets stood along one wall. She swiftly picked the locks and flipped through the folders. In the bottom drawer of one cabinet she found visitor sign-in sheets. There were hundreds of them.

She glanced over to check on the transmission, then went back to the visitor logs. There appeared to be a separate sheet for every shift on every day.

"Evergreen," she said, "can you give me the dates of Jing's visits? The paper logs are extensive."

"Just a minute, Phoenix."

Sydney watched the lights on the code breaker while she waited, willing it to go faster. Over the comm, she heard Dixon and his guests commenting on the meal.

Minutes dragged by as Sydney scanned through the logs. They were a mixture of Japanese and English signatures, each one time-stamped and initialed by the guard on duty, and each entry listed the visitor's name and destination.

Even if Jing wasn't a resident, or used a different name, they could easily track his activity. All they had to do was locate the few significant pages in the thousands of sheets in the file.

"Phoenix, I've got it." As Nadia read the dates, Sydney grabbed the corresponding week's folder from the file drawer. She had a stack of five folders on the floor when she again heard footsteps approaching.

She slid the drawer closed and hid the files in her bag before ducking back behind the desk.

This time, the steps paused outside the door and a key rattled in the lock. Sydney switched on her scanner, finding a single person outside.

"I've got company," she whispered.

The door swung open. Sydney turned off the scanner and slid the glasses off.

A single security guard stepped into the room, the door swinging shut behind him. He glanced around, as though reassuring himself the room was empty.

The guard headed back toward the door, and Syd relaxed a fraction. But he caught sight of the red linen coat and turned around. He looked at the desk, where the code breaker continued to flash and blink.

The guard approached the desk, reaching for the code breaker.

Sydney leaped from her hiding place, grabbed the guard by one arm, and swung him around, away from the desk.

He stumbled into her, shouting. Syd jabbed her fingers into his throat, stopping him in mid-cry.

The guard's hands clutched at his throat and he gasped for air, finally drawing a deep, ragged breath.

Syd glanced at the code breaker, still blinking.

"Evergreen, how far are we?"

"Seventy-seven percent, Phoenix. We need a couple more minutes."

"Great," Sydney muttered.

The guard pulled a nine-millimeter automatic from his holster. Spinning, she used her momentum to kick the gun from his hand.

"Wonderful!" Dixon said again, acknowledging he had heard their exchange.

The guard tried to yell as the gun spun away, but it came out as a raspy yelp. He leaped at Sydney.

Sydney stepped back and kicked out again. Her foot connected with the guard's knee, sending him to the floor.

"Evergreen?"

"Eighty-four percent, Phoenix."

Sydney reached for her bag, but the guard grabbed her ankle and tried to trip her. She slipped, then wrenched her ankle from his grasp.

Sydney was pulled off balance. She stumbled forward, smacked her hip painfully on the corner of the desk, and fell against the chair. She deliberately fell farther forward, tumbled over the chair, and somersaulted to her feet on the far side. She spun around, sliding her gaze past the flashing code breaker.

The guard was on his feet, scrambling toward his gun.

"Eighty-seven percent," Nadia reported.

"Wonderful," Dixon said.

Sydney launched herself across the room. She planted one foot on the guard's back and smashed his head against the floor.

"My guest is taking a little nap," Sydney said.

"But I am sure he has friends who will come looking for him soon."

"Eighty-nine percent complete," Nadia replied.

Sydney yanked a pair of handcuffs from the
guard's heavy leather belt. She pulled his arms
behind his back and shackled his wrists together.

She glanced around the room and saw a wide
satin sash on the display of sales awards. She
pulled it off the wall and tied it around the unconscious guard's mouth, gagging him.

"Ninety-two percent."

Sydney took one last look around the room. The
guard lay unmoving. The file drawers were closed
and she quickly fastened the locks into place. The
folders she needed were in her bag.

A movement on one of the monitors caught her
attention, and she looked up to see Dixon's two
companions standing up.

"Stall them, Outrigger," Sydney said. "I need a
couple more minutes."

Dixon stayed in his chair, delaying their
departure.

Sydney remembered her search. "Chocolate!"
she said. "Ask for chocolate."

"This was wonderful," Dixon said, waving his

hand over the table, now littered with tiny plates that had held their lunch. "But I would really like something sweet to finish it off, wouldn't you?"

The two men remained standing, as though anxious to begin their tour. But Dixon remained deliberately oblivious to their body language and leaned back in his chair.

"Do you think the kitchen can bring us something chocolate?" he asked.

Sydney glanced between the code breaker and the monitor. She saw the salesman hesitate at the word chocolate. She had guessed right about the stash in the drawer.

"Ninety-eight percent," Nadia said.

The guard stirred and tried to roll over. Sydney pulled a delicate gold atomizer from her purse and twisted the bulb. One quick spritz from the hidden reservoir, and his eyes rolled back in his head.

"Done!" Nadia cried.

Sydney rolled up the plastic code breaker and stuffed it into her bag. She replaced the keyboard, though she doubted it would make any difference. The sleeping guard would be evidence enough that the building's security had been breached.

"Outrigger, I'm moving," Sydney said. She put

her coat back on, flipped her sunglasses down, and checked through the door before easing it open.

Within minutes, she was on the street, hailing a taxi. As she rode toward the safe house, she listened to Dixon manufacturing outrage over some perceived slight and extricating himself from the disappointed salesman.

By the time Sydney finally reached the safe house, Nadia had already uplinked the file to Marshall.

While they waited for Dixon to make his way back, the three agents took the files from the building and began to correlate the written record with the video surveillance logs.

It was late afternoon, and Dixon was stuck in rush hour traffic. From the backseat of the creeping taxi, he called the safe house, using a cell phone Marshall had prepared.

"It works for a single call," Marshall had said. "Three minutes, tops. Then the circuits fuse and it can't be used again. Just make your call—Hi, Mom? It's Marshall. Your son? You know—" He had stopped short and handed the phone to Dixon. "Anyway, one call per phone. There's a dozen of them in the mission supplies."

At the safe house, Sydney answered the phone.

"What have you found?" Dixon asked.

"Not much." Disappointment was clear in Sydney's voice.

The team was certain Jing was in Tokyo, along with Peotr Alexyeev. But they were only two people in a city of more than twelve million. Finding them was a daunting task.

Sydney continued as Dixon crept through traffic. "Merlin is working on the files, but so far, nothing. Same with the hard copy. Maybe we'll have more by the time you get back."

"Another half hour at least," Dixon said. "I may just give up and walk."

When Dixon arrived, the rest of the team was sitting at the small kitchen table, staring at security logs. Sydney gestured to an empty chair and invited him to sit down.

"We've been through these things twice," she said. "We've tied the sign-in times to the video surveillance, and compared the video time stamp with the paper logs. According to our records, Jing was only there once."

"The tape shows at least three visits," Dixon said. "Maybe more."

"We cross-checked," Weiss said. "If that was him all three times, he didn't use the same name."

"Wait a minute." Sydney grabbed the sheets, looking at the headings this time rather than the signatures. "Look at this," she said, pointing to the names on the top of the pages. "Every visit occurs when a different security guard is on duty."

"So?" Weiss took the papers from her, looking at the data to confirm.

"Don't you see?" Sydney pointed. "The visits were timed so that no guard would see him more than once." She selected three sheets of paper and spread them on the table. "Here." She pointed. "And here." She pointed again. "And here."

The agents looked closely at the signature on each of the sign-in sheets. Although the name was different each time, all the names were written with English characters, and the handwriting was similar.

Weiss looked from one sheet to the next. "But he's listed as visiting a different tenant each time," he said.

"Let's put Marshall on it," Nadia suggested. "See if he can find a link between the three tenants in the files we sent him."

Sydney nodded. "I'll take care of that."

Nadia stood and stretched. "I need to get dressed." She nodded at Weiss. "We should be going soon."

Weiss glanced up at Nadia and smiled. Even though they were on assignment, he was obviously enjoying the opportunity to spend time with her.

Sydney was happy for her sister and Weiss, pleased that the two of them were developing a friendship that hinted at becoming something more. They were part of the network of friends and family that surrounded her.

She felt a faint shiver of guilt over her own comfort as she watched the lights of the city emerge from the gathering darkness. Peotr Alexyeev was being held hostage out there somewhere, with no friends and no family. It was up to Sydney and her team to find him. Find him and free him from Jing's captivity.

But for what?

So Arvin Sloane could lock him up and put him to work? Trade one jailer for another? Sydney was still not sure she could trust Sloane with the knowledge Alexyeev carried in his head. It was a question she knew she would have to confront when they found Alexyeev.

She was already thinking about ignoring Sloane's orders, and she realized she had been since the beginning. Alexyeev was a valuable asset to whoever had access to him. But who could be trusted with that kind of knowledge?

CHAPTER 22

Sydney watched her sister emerge from the bedroom and stifled a laugh at Weiss's reaction. Nadia wore skintight black leather pants and spike-heeled boots. A silky, pale peach camisole accentuated her dusky shoulders.

Weiss seemed to be having trouble swallowing.

Sydney caught Dixon's eye, and he grinned, sharing the brief flash of amusement. Reasons to smile were often few and far between, and Sydney welcomed the brief respite.

Nadia covered her bare arms and shoulders

with a black satin bomber jacket, and Weiss finally managed to speak.

"I'd say don't wait up for us," he joked, "but that's your job."

Dixon and Sydney waited until Nadia and Weiss reached the street. They were taking the subway to the Ginza district, and Sydney and Dixon were following in the team's van as backup.

Dixon drove through the crowded Tokyo streets, snaking south with the lines of traffic, until they reached the glittering Ginza.

They drove slowly and eventually found a parking space near Hibiya Park, a popular spot across from the elegant Imperial Hotel.

"Evergreen, Houdini," Dixon said, "this is Outrigger. We're here if you need us."

"Roger," Weiss replied.

The YZ Club was one of the hottest spots in the Ginza. Weiss paid the steep cover charge and followed Nadia into the packed main room of the club.

Lights strobed through the darkness, flashing across a tangle of waving arms on the dance floor. Tables were packed around the sides of the room with a group of fashionably dressed young people ringing each one.

"I don't know," Weiss said. "This doesn't look like Jing's kind of crowd."

Nadia leaned close, shouting to be heard over the pulsing music. "I know. But this is the place Marshall said. Let's at least have a look around."

Weiss nodded and wrapped his arm around Nadia's shoulders. He told himself it was just to keep them from getting separated in the crowd, but that didn't stop him from enjoying it.

"Outrigger, this is Merlin. Are you there?" Marshall's voice came over the link from L.A.

"I'm here, Merlin. What have you got?"

"We just got a hit. Somebody bought a round of drinks in the YZ Club."

"Roger that, Merlin," Dixon acknowledged.

At the same time, Sydney spoke into the comm. "Evergreen, Houdini, Merlin informs us someone just bought a round of drinks on Jing's account. He's got to be there somewhere."

"Roger that, Phoenix," Nadia replied. "Does Merlin have any other information?"

Sydney glanced at Dixon, who shook his head. "Negative, Evergreen. That's all we have so far."

Weiss and Nadia exchanged a look and moved in opposite directions, scanning the tables for a fresh round of drinks and a familiar face.

The club was extremely warm, and Nadia let her jacket slide off her shoulders. She hooked one finger in the collar and slung it over her shoulder as she made her way around the outside of the dance floor.

She had to fend off repeated offers to buy her a drink and numerous invitations to dance. Each time, she smiled and murmured that she was meeting someone. She kept moving, never pausing long enough to engage in actual conversation.

One man, a little older than the rest of the crowd, tried to follow her. He was insistent that she dance with him. When she wouldn't, he grabbed her jacket, pulling her back as she tried to walk away.

Nadia whirled around and faced the man. A swift glance told her they were unobserved, and an equally swift move left him with a dislocated thumb and an overwhelming desire to get as far away from her as possible.

"Evergreen, you okay?" Weiss said over the comm.

"The gentleman had too much to drink," Nadia replied. "I encouraged him to go home and sleep it off." She quickly changed the subject. "Any sign of Jing?"

"Not yet." Weiss sighed. "But I'll keep looking."

"Evergreen," Sydney said, "is there a problem?"

"Negative," Nadia replied. "Just a guy who didn't want to take no for an answer. Nothing important."

Sydney couldn't help but grin. Her sister might be small, but she was more than a match for any man.

Meanwhile, Weiss had circled the floor without spotting any sign of Jing. He turned down a hallway leading to the restrooms. Partway along the hall was a staircase. A sign in Japanese indicated it led to a private lounge.

"Evergreen, I'm going upstairs."

"Be careful," Nadia replied. "That's private."

"I know," Weiss said. "But I don't read Japanese. Just a dumb American tourist with more money than sense, right?"

Weiss climbed the stairs to the balcony level, expecting a challenge at any minute. But no one appeared.

At the top, a small landing looked over the main floor. On each side of the landing, heavy curtains led to private rooms that shared the same view. Weiss hesitated, looking from one set of curtains to the other. He could enter one room, but not both.

"Evergreen, there are two private rooms up here. I can't hear over the music, but the curtains are closed, and I think there are people in both. Can you see anything from down there?"

Nadia craned her neck and looked up at the balcony. In the darkness, all she could see were the tiny bright spots of candles flickering on the tables.

"Nothing that helps. Candle lights in both rooms. Wait. Someone moved in the left room. I think he's headed your way."

Before she finished speaking, a wide man in a loud sport shirt and heavy gold chains pushed aside the curtains on Weiss's left. He stopped when he saw the agent.

"This is private," he said in Japanese.

Weiss looked at the man and shook his head.

"Private," the man repeated, a hard edge in his voice.

Weiss shrugged and smiled. "Nice place," he said, in a flat Midwestern accent. "Really nice. Don't have anything like this back in Omaha."

The man stared hard for a moment, and Weiss

waved toward the curtained room. "Can I get a drink in there? It's so crowded downstairs." He glanced toward the dance floor below. "I couldn't even get the waiter's attention."

The man glared. Weiss was certain the man understood him but wasn't going to reply in English.

Weiss took a step toward the open curtain, straining to see into the gloom. There was a small group in the room, and Weiss could see someone who resembled Jing. The broad man stepped between Weiss and the door.

"Is that Jackie Chan?" Weiss said, hoping the team would understand. "It looks like Jackie Chan, I swear to God."

Nadia spoke over the comm. "You found him?"

"I'd swear that is Jackie Chan," Weiss said in answer.

"On my way," Sydney and Nadia said at the same time.

Weiss stood his ground for another minute, craning his neck to see into the room.

He played the part of a rubbernecking tourist, giving the rest of the team time to move into position.

As Nadia approached the bottom of the stairs,

he pulled out his wallet. He took out a fat packet of one-thousand-yen notes and shoved them at the man. "My wife will never forgive me if I don't get his autograph," he said. He added another wad of notes. "Just one autograph, I swear."

The bodyguard stiff-armed Weiss and took the money. He balled it up and shoved it into the front of Weiss's shirt.

"Private," he repeated in Japanese.

"Is that a no?" Weiss said with a note of indignation. "What, you want American money?"

Weiss took a wad of fifty-dollar bills from his pocket and held them out. "Is this what you want?"

The bodyguard's face contorted with anger.

"Evergreen in position," Nadia said.

"Phoenix ready."

"Outrigger ready."

The team was in place. It was time to leave.

Weiss snatched his hand back and stuffed the money into his pocket. "Okay, buddy. If that's the way you want it."

He stepped back toward the stairs and shouted in the direction of the room. "But I'm coming back with my wife. You wouldn't treat a lady this way. Jackie's a gentleman, I know it; he'll give her an autograph." He hesitated, then added his parting shot. "And I'm not ever watching another one of your movies!"

The big man stepped toward Weiss. He reached out with one meaty hand and grabbed the front of Weiss's shirt. With one jerk, he popped the buttons, sending thousand-yen notes drifting to the floor. Then he shoved Weiss down the stairs.

Weiss twisted, falling against the railing. He grabbed the handrail and managed to stop his descent. When he looked back up, the bodyguard was calmly picking up the money.

At the bottom of the stairs, Nadia was waiting. "Outrigger is bringing the van, and Phoenix is covering the front," she said.

Weiss nodded. He followed Nadia out of the club and around the back, where a heavy security door marked the rear exit from the club. They moved down the alley a few feet, past a waiting limousine.

Nadia wrapped her arms around Weiss and stumbled against him. Hibiya Park had the reputation of a lovers' lane, and an amorous couple was a common sight near the park.

The limousine driver had his window down a

few inches, cigarette smoke snaking from the narrow opening. As they passed his door, Nadia heard a knowing chuckle from inside.

Once past the limo, they turned the corner and stopped. Nadia's black clothing made her nearly invisible in the dark alleyway as she peeked back around the corner.

The limo idled in the alley, the smell of its exhaust mingling with the odor of grease coming from the kitchen vents.

They didn't have to wait long. The door opened and the bodyguard emerged first. Jing followed a few steps behind with a young woman at his side. They both appeared intoxicated, and the bodyguard was trying to shepherd them into the waiting limousine.

"Phoenix, Outrigger, they're here," Weiss said. "Evergreen and Houdini are in play."

The driver got out of the limo and opened the door. The bodyguard stood to one side, letting Jing and his companion go past him. He looked up and down the alley, as though waiting for trouble.

"I'll take the bodyguard," Weiss said. "I owe him one."

"Phoenix here," Sydney said. "I have the end of the alley."

"Outrigger in position," Dixon said. "Go!"

Nadia moved in on the driver, who turned to run. She caught him before he had gone more than a couple of steps and jumped on his back, wrapping one arm around his neck.

Weiss ran directly at the bodyguard, moving fast and low. The man was big, but he was a bruiser, used to intimidating others with his size alone. He went down as Weiss hit him at the knees with a perfect tackle.

Weiss grunted with satisfaction as the bodyguard ricocheted off the side of the heavily armored limousine. There was a loud crack as his head hit the fender, and the guard's body went slack. Weiss turned his attention to Jing and his companion.

The driver struggled, trying to throw Nadia off. There was no place to conceal a weapon in her skintight pants and skimpy top, but she produced a tiny can of Mace from her jacket pocket.

Ducking her head, she slammed the can against the man's chest, breaking the seal and releasing the painful gas.

The driver fell to the ground, Nadia forgotten, as he clawed at the tears running down his face.

Nadia whirled to confront Jing. Weiss had one

of Jing's arms twisted behind his back, but the girl who was with him was hitting Weiss over the head with her purse. She was also screaming, a high, piercing shriek that cut through Nadia.

Nadia grabbed the girl, wrenching her purse out of her hand and throwing it down the alley. "Shut up!" she commanded in Japanese.

The girl collapsed onto the broken pavement, whimpering and moaning. "Please don't kill me," she said over and over, her drunken shrieking now reduced to a pitiful whine.

The bodyguard was beginning to stir.

Nadia shoved the girl into the back of the limo, out of her way. She stepped over the writhing driver and clocked the bodyguard in the back of the head with a loose brick from the alley. Crude, but effective.

Headlights pierced the end of the alley, and Nadia heard a vehicle rushing toward them. The driver staggered to his feet and stood up, waving desperately.

Tires squealed as the van rocked to a stop.

Dixon jumped from the driver's seat. The limo driver rushed at him, babbling that he was being robbed.

Dixon extended his arm and the driver stopped. The agent had hit him with a tranquilizer gun.

Sydney was right behind Dixon. She grabbed the driver as he fell, dragging him into the back of the van.

Weiss shoved Jing into the back of the limo with his terrified companion. While Dixon covered the captives with his Sig Sauer, Weiss and Nadia handcuffed them.

Between them, Dixon and Weiss managed to drag the bodyguard into the back of the van with the unconscious driver.

Seconds later, the van left the alley with the limousine following it.

A short while later, the two vehicles pulled over in a deserted industrial area. Jing and the woman were transferred to the van, which Dixon and Sydney took to the safe house.

Nadia and Weiss searched the limo but found nothing. They quickly cleaned it and parked it near a subway station before taking the train back to the safe house.

When they arrived, Dixon and Sydney had the van in the garage with the door securely locked.

In the subbasement, Jing and the drunken girl were strapped to chairs. The girl still whimpered occasionally. But Jing neither moved nor spoke.

The driver was in the basement. Dixon had washed his eyes and applied a soothing ointment. A bandage was wound around his head, holding compresses over his eyes.

The bodyguard was still unconscious and had been left in the van. Sturdy chains were looped around his ankles and wrists and secured to eye-bolts in the van floor.

They decided to question the girl first.

Nadia removed her restraints, led her up the stairs to the basement, and strapped her into a comfortable chair. The girl tearfully accepted the offer of tea. The cup Nadia handed her contained tea and a powerful stimulant, designed to burn off the effects of alcohol in a matter of minutes.

Sydney and Dixon watched from a surveillance room. Monitors displayed video of Jing, sitting motionless in the subbasement; Nadia in the basement room with the girl; the silent van in the garage; and Weiss, sitting with the sleeping driver.

Nadia waited for the drug to work before she asked any questions. But even sober, the girl was either incredibly frightened or a consummate actress.

After a few minutes, Nadia left the girl alone and joined the rest of the team.

"Her identity checks out," Sydney said. "She's a clerk in a downtown boutique. She supports her partying with the occasional 'date,' but we didn't find anything else."

"So what she said—about picking up Jing because he had a lot of money—was true?" Nadia asked.

Dixon nodded. "The sensors confirm it. Unless she can beat a functional imaging test, she's telling the truth."

Nadia made a disgusted noise. "All that, for a party girl!"

Nadia took over in the surveillance room while Dixon and Sydney went to the subbasement to confront Jing. They had let him stew long enough.

Now it was time for some answers.

CHAPTER 23

Sydney and Dixon got answers.

They just weren't the answers they had expected.

Jing watched them walk into the room. His date might have been intoxicated, but he was not. He was clearly sober and very relaxed, given that he was shackled to a chair.

He didn't say a word.

Dixon and Sydney walked around their prisoner. He followed them with his eyes until they stepped behind him, out of his field of vision. He didn't turn his head.

"We know you have Alexyeev," Sydney said.

"They take kidnapping very seriously in Russia," Dixon added, "especially when the victim is a respected scientist."

They continued circling Jing in opposite directions, so that he couldn't see them both at once.

"Tell us where he is," Dixon said in korean.

"I can't."

"I think you can," Dixon said smoothly. "In fact, I think you'll want to, very quickly."

"I can't," he repeated, "even if I do want to. I can't tell you what I don't know."

"You kidnapped a top genetic scientist," Sydney said, "and you can't *remember* where you put him? People don't forget things like that, Jing."

"True. And if I had this man, this Alex whatever, I would know where he is. But since I do not have him, I cannot tell you what you want to know."

Sydney whirled and faced Jing. She moved close, bending over so her face was level with Jing's. "You will tell us—eventually—because if you do, life will be a little more bearable. And if you don't"—her voice was lower, almost a growl—"you will wish you had never been born."

Jing paused, as though considering her words. "I believe you," he said. "Really, I do. But you can't get what isn't mine, even that name."

"What name?" Dixon asked, moving in behind Sydney. "What name don't you have?"

"Jing."

Sydney just stared at him. "You expect me to believe that? We should just say, oh, we're sorry, because you refuse to admit your identity?"

"No, I expect you to do just what you are doing. I expect you not to believe me. I do look like Colonel Jing—now."

Sydney leaned in, looking closely at the man's face. She was within a couple of inches before she could see the scars.

Faint lines ran along the man's nose and mouth. If she hadn't been looking for them, she would have thought they were the first signs of aging. But looking closely, they were scars, the marks of a skilled surgeon.

The man looked steadily at Sydney. "Do you know the word 'doppelgänger'? That's me. A lot of very delicate work. Very *good* work, but ultimately only a copy."

The man smiled at her, in a way that made her

skin crawl. "You can test my blood if you'd like. They weren't able to alter that."

Sydney turned away and looked at Dixon. They had been duped. They would do the tests, but she already knew what the results would be. He wasn't Jing. And whoever he actually was, this copy didn't have the one thing they needed: Jing's secrets.

Dixon's eyes widened, and he pushed past her, reaching for their prisoner. The man's face contorted, and he gasped for breath. The odor of bitter almonds seeped from his mouth.

"Cyanide!" Dixon cried.

Sydney rushed to the supply cabinet. She pawed through the shelves and found an emergency oxygen supply, which she tossed to Dixon. She continued looking until she found amyl nitrite pearls. They might not be enough, but it was all she had.

The records from the high-rise had yielded nothing new, but Marshall continued searching.

Their prisoner from the club was comatose, unable to answer questions, but he had survived his suicide attempt. It was only a matter of time— time they didn't have—before they could question him again.

They were convinced he knew something. Why else would he try to kill himself?

The driver and bodyguard were hired through a temporary service agency. They didn't know anything, so the two of them, along with the party girl, were spirited out of Tokyo by local contacts. By the time they returned, any story they might tell would be discredited.

Marshall uplinked a series of maps and satellite surveillance photos of their next target. They showed a tight cluster of industrial buildings just off the Wangan Expressway, at the edge of Tokyo Bay.

Sydney and Dixon took the van as soon as it was dark and headed south on the Shuto Expressway.

Land in Tokyo was scarce, and over the years precious acres had been reclaimed from the ocean. The manufactured land sat in neat blocks of islands, connected by a web of bridges and tunnels. As they turned east onto Odaiba Island, Sydney caught sight of the gleaming inverted pyramids of Tokyo Big Sight, the exhibition center.

The district appeared to be undergoing a revival. There were shops and restaurants that were no more than a few years old and luxury hotels clustered around the exhibition center.

Dixon left the expressway, and the glittering neon of fashionable shopping and dining disappeared behind them.

As they drove, the streets grew narrower and darker, lined with industrial buildings closed for the night. They stopped a few blocks from the building Marshall had indicated and parked the van.

From there, they would travel on foot.

"This is Phoenix," Sydney said. "We are in play."

Sydney's scanning glasses didn't function well in the low light, but she and Dixon both carried infrared goggles. They moved cautiously through the deserted streets, staying in the shadows of the buildings.

Their progress was nearly silent as they crept toward their target. Marshall had identified a windowless warehouse set near the water as a suspected site.

In the darkness ahead of her, Sydney heard a noise. She stopped, holding her breath, still and silent. She waited for the noise to come again, but there was nothing. She held her position for a long ten count, then raised her infrared goggles and looked around.

She could see Dixon's heat signature a few yards ahead on the opposite side of the street. There was another faint blur around the corner of the building. Too small for a human, it was probably a cat or a rat. She ignored it and moved on.

The target building was surrounded by a bare parking lot that offered no cover as they approached. Sydney and Dixon stopped in the shelter of a cluster of trees.

According to Marshall, there were surveillance cameras at regular intervals around the building, but the cameras couldn't see the building itself, only the surroundings. It was time for Marshall to do his magic.

"Merlin, this is Phoenix. We're ready for a little blackout here."

In Los Angeles, Marshall flexed his fingers and poised them over his keyboard. "Okay, Phoenix. The emergency power system is designed to take over after ten seconds. I'll try to get you more than that, but assume you'll have ten seconds, no more. The exterior building lights are on emergency power, but not the parking lot. Stand by."

Sydney and Dixon braced themselves to run across the lot.

"Outrigger, Phoenix, get ready. Blackout in five, four, three, two, one."

The building and the parking lot went dark.

Dixon rushed across the lot, Sydney at his heels. Dixon reached the side of the building just as the lights flickered on. He flattened himself against the wall, breathing hard.

Sydney was a few steps behind him. When the lights came on, she was forced to duck behind one of the few cars in the lot.

The lot lights stayed out, but she was trapped. She couldn't cross the illuminated strip of empty ground without being seen.

"Merlin," she hissed. "I need more time."

"Emergency power is already on," he answered. "Give me a minute to see what I can do."

A vehicle approached, its lights sweeping the lot as it turned off the street. For a moment, it was hidden from view by a maintenance building. Dixon took advantage of the break. He slid along the side of the building and disappeared around the far end.

"Wait, Merlin," Sydney said. "There's a car coming."

She slid under the parked car, flattening herself against the asphalt. It smelled of motor oil. Dust tickled her nose, and she pinched it, fighting the need to sneeze.

The car approached, its lights swinging across the nearly empty parking lot. It circled the lot twice, slowly, then stopped next to the building, engine idling.

After a few seconds, the car pulled away, the driver apparently satisfied.

Sydney waited until the taillights disappeared onto the street before she crawled back out from under the parked car.

"All clear, Merlin," she reported. "Now would be a good time."

"Roger, Phoenix. Lights out in three, two, one."

Once again, the lot was plunged into darkness.

"Outrigger, I'm headed your way."

Sydney ran straight for the far corner of the building, beyond which Dixon waited in the dark.

There was a man-high loading dock at the end of the building, facing the water. The dock itself was dim, with emergency battery lights casting weak, yellow light across the empty space.

Sydney ran her hands along the edge of the

loading dock until she found what she was looking for: a pressure switch designed to activate the loading alarm. It was a weak point in the security system that provided access to the entire network.

With Dixon's help, she tapped into the switch, connecting an override monitor. The monitor began downloading security codes, beaming them via satellite to Marshall's waiting computer.

For two long minutes, they stood in the shadow of the loading dock, watching the faint red signal lights flash. Seconds ticked past with agonizing slowness.

Over the comm, Sydney could hear Marshall muttering to himself as he worked. "Reroute the signal . . . link that feed . . . loop it back . . . select the input . . ." The muttering stopped. A few more seconds ticked past.

The signal light flashed green. At the same time, they heard Marshall's triumphant "Yes!" over the comm.

"You're clear to go, Outrigger. Good luck!"

Dixon and Sydney scrambled up the concrete stairs at the side of the loading platform.

The wide double doors were held closed with heavy deadbolts. While Sydney worked on the locks, Dixon scanned for sounds of activity within the building.

"Anything, Outrigger?" Sydney asked.

"The walls are reinforced against electronic surveillance," Dixon replied. He looked at the display on the scanner. "The signal can't get past their jammers."

"Even with the alarms down?" Syd felt another tumbler click into place.

"Afraid so," Dixon said. "We'll be going in blind."

"Then let's hope our intel is accurate. There isn't supposed to be anybody in there at night."

The last tumbler fell into place, and the doors moved lightly on their well-oiled hinges.

Sydney looked at Dixon. In the dim light his face was little more than a shadow. He made a thumbs-up gesture and pushed the door open.

Sydney followed him in, the two agents moving in opposite directions, weapons drawn.

They were in a large room, clearly intended for shipping and receiving. The center of the room was filled by a large shipping counter, with a package scale to one side. Only a few low-wattage security lights were lit, and the room danced with eerie shadows.

"Merlin, this is Outrigger," Dixon said. "So far, so good." He crossed the room to a pair of swinging doors.

Dixon paused, listening. Sydney circled the room and stood behind him. Satisfied the corridor was empty, Dixon went through the door with Sydney behind him.

They were on the production floor of a manufacturing plant that had been idle for a long time. The machinery was still in place, but there were no materials, no tools, nothing to indicate that anyone had been in the plant in months, or maybe even years. Some of the machines were covered with tarps.

At the far end of the production floor, a series of offices formed a short hallway. The upper half of each wall was glass, offering the office workers a permanent view of the factory. Through the glass walls, Sydney could see that all the rooms were empty.

"Looks deserted," Sydney said. "Merlin, you sure this is the place?"

"Phoenix, this is Raptor." Sydney was startled to hear her father's voice instead of Marshall's. "We're positive."

Sydney nodded, even though she knew her father couldn't see her. "Roger that, Raptor. We'll keep looking."

Just past the offices, a wall separated the production area from the rest of the building. An unlocked door opened onto a carpeted lobby with wood paneling and recessed lighting.

The lobby was open and airy, even though it had no windows. Walls of backlit glass brick gave the illusion of natural light. A dramatic off-center staircase behind a security desk emphasized the high ceiling.

The staircase led to a mezzanine level, where a deep balcony hung over one side of the room. At the other end of the balcony was a single door, its stark, blond wood face nearly invisible against the adjoining paneling. It was the only other exit from the lobby.

They climbed the staircase and moved along the balcony.

As Sydney and Dixon approached the door, they found signs that someone else had been there recently. A discarded soda can, condensation still clinging to its side, had been dropped carelessly on the floor. In the wall next to the door was another, much smaller door. Moving cautiously, Dixon reached out with a slender probe and slowly levered it open.

Inside it was a card reader and a numerical keypad. When the tiny door opened, a projected image of kanji characters sprang to life across the larger door.

Sydney read the words, quickly translating them into English. "Warning: active biological specimens. No entry without prior approval. Violations will result in immediate dismissal."

Dixon made a disgusted noise. "I think we know how Mr. Jing defines dismissal."

"There's another security system, Raptor," Sydney reported. "We'll need to bypass it in order to get beyond this door."

"Roger, Phoenix. Let me know if there is anything we can do to be of assistance."

APO HEADQUARTERS
LOS ANGELES

Marshall Flinkman rubbed the bridge of his nose. His eyes felt like sandpaper. He had been staring at Alexyeev's notes for days. Hacking the security codes for the warehouse had been a welcome break, but Jack Bristow had taken over the mission, and Marshall was back to code breaking.

Most of the notes had been translated, and he had most of the code decrypted, but one passage still eluded him. It seemed to refer to Alexyeev's wife, which didn't make sense.

The code was complex, and Marshall found it easier to work on it directly, rather than writing a computer algorithm.

But it was much harder on his eyes. Although he was working from the translations, he sometimes had to go back to Alexyeev's original notes, in his small, tight handwriting.

He linked two pieces of code. The result unlocked another page of notes, and he read through them rapidly. His heart beat faster as he read, confirming information they had only guessed at up until now.

Marshall reread the passage about Alexyeev's wife, and his eyes grew wide. Abandoning his work, he raced into the conference room, where Jack was talking to Sydney and Dixon in Tokyo.

"We were right about the mutation," Marshall said. "The virus changes with every transmission." He stopped.

Sydney's voice came from the comm link.

"I've got the second digit. Three to go."

"She can't go in there!"

Jack frowned at Marshall. "What do you mean?"

"Sydney, she's a girl. She can't go in the laboratory, not if they think Alexyeev might be in there. There is an X-chromosome link within the viral protein. See, in the human genome there are twenty-two common pairs of chromosomes, and then there's the X and Y, and females have two X-chromosomes, and males—"

Jack held up a hand. "English!" he barked. "Now!"

"Third digit," Sydney said.

"The virus thrives on uterine tissue. Women are much more susceptible."

"Abort the mission. Repeat. Abort the mission," Jack said. "Phoenix, I want you out of there—now! I'll explain later."

CHAPTER 24

ODAIBA ISLAND
TOKYO, JAPAN

Sydney wanted to argue. They had hit so many dead ends. Now they had reached what looked like the right place, and Jack was calling her off.

"Come on," Dixon said. "You heard the man. Let's go."

Dixon moved toward the stairs, but Sydney hesitated.

"Now, Phoenix! Get out of there!" It was as if Jack could see her wavering, from thousands of miles away.

The urgency and concern in her father's voice

311

was clear. Sydney reluctantly complied. *He better have a good reason.*

She stuffed her equipment in her pack and ran down the stairs after Dixon.

They shot through the door into the factory area, sprinted across the production floor, and went out the double doors onto the loading dock.

The night was still and peaceful. In the distance, she could see the lights of the towering Ferris wheel in the commercial center of Odaiba Island.

The override monitor was still attached to the pressure switch.

"Raptor," Sydney said, "is Merlin there?"

"Right here, Phoenix," Marshall answered. "How can I help?"

"Can we disconnect the override monitor?"

"Let's see. If you do, the circuit will reset, but it will have to cycle up, so there's the reboot time, plus system refresh, plus link . . . I'd say you'll have about twenty-two seconds before the cameras are back online."

"We can do that," Dixon said. "And I'd rather we didn't leave a calling card."

Sydney relocked the doors to the loading dock.

They worked together to remove the override monitor and reconnect the security system. Syd twisted the last pair of wires together and shoved the switch back into place.

"Go!" Dixon said.

They didn't slow down until they were a block away from the warehouse.

Sydney looked back over her shoulder at the dark bulk of the building against the night sky. The building was empty, with the possible exception of the room they had not entered. If Alexyeev was there, he might be the only person in the entire cavernous structure. Just as he had been the only person in the bunker in North Korea.

And if they were right, he was a prisoner. He had been forced into isolation, held against his will.

And would turning him over to Sloane make that any different?

Back on the expressway, headed for the safe house, Sydney asked her father for an explanation.

"It's complicated, Phoenix. Just go back to the apartment and wait. Get some rest. Shotgun is already on his way with new supplies and instructions. You'll have your answers in a few hours. Raptor out."

APO HEADQUARTERS
LOS ANGELES, CALIFORNIA

Jack Bristow broke the connection with his daughter. He still could feel the fear that had gripped him when Marshall had explained the danger Sydney was in. He hadn't let the fear make his decision, however. The danger to everyone was very real, and unleashing the virus without proper controls could spread disease and panic with alarming speed.

"Explain to me again what you found in those journals," he said, turning to Marshall. "I want to know everything there is to know before the team goes near Alexyeev."

Marshall was calmer, now that Sydney was out of immediate danger. "The journals are records of Alexyeev's disease, which we already knew. The disease was the result of the Alliance bioweapons program. But infection required physical contact, some exchange of fluids—blood, saliva, a drop of sweat.

"Anyway, the Alliance abandoned the project. The virus was often lethal, but it couldn't be spread easily, so it wasn't what they wanted. Alexyeev was out of a job, but he had become a carrier. According to his journals, the disease went into random periods of remission. He was never sick, just more infectious or less infectious. When he discovered the X-chromosome link, he worried about his wife, but she was immune. Unfortunately, his children weren't. He speculated that the genetic key that protected his wife made his daughters hypersensitive. He was working on an antidote based on her genetic chemistry when she committed suicide."

Jack shook his head. "We better bring Sloane up to speed on this. We've got a human time bomb sitting in that warehouse—if that's where he is— and we don't even know how much time is left before it goes off."

APO SAFE HOUSE
TOKYO, JAPAN

Sydney sat on the edge of the futon in the living room of the Tokyo safe house. Dixon and Weiss had pulled chairs up near her, and Nadia sat beside her.

"And he didn't tell you anything else?" Nadia asked.

Sydney shook her head. "He told me to wait for Vaughn to get here with new supplies and new instructions. But how can we just sit here when we know Alexyeev is out there, somewhere in this city, and he could start an epidemic?"

Nadia reached over and patted her sister's arm. "Trust him, Sydney. He does know what he's doing. He wants this to be over as much as you do."

Sydney leaned back and crossed her arms over her chest, hugging herself. "Can we at least keep a watch on the building?"

Weiss shook his head. "According to Sloane, the local field office is doing just that. And they've tasked a satellite to track any movement in or out of the building. If anything happens, we'll know about it."

Sydney nodded. She stifled her irritation, but the irony of her situation provided a moment of bitter amusement. Once again, she was waiting for Michael Vaughn.

By the time Vaughn arrived, Sydney had slept, but she still wanted answers. The ones Vaughn gave her weren't reassuring.

When he had finished summarizing the new information, they didn't have many questions left, except who would be on the team for the next visit to the warehouse.

"There are only two doses of the antiviral," Vaughn said, "which means if we treat both of you"—he glanced at Sydney and Nadia—"we won't have any backup. The lab has been working around the clock, but they haven't been able to synthesize the compound. Alexyeev hadn't figured it out either. Without his wife's DNA, of which he had only a small sample, he couldn't solve the puzzle. And he'd been working on it for years."

"I'll go," Nadia said, firmly.

"No. This is my mission. I've been in there before. I know the layout and the security codes." Sydney spoke in a determined and commanding tone, one that reminded Vaughn of her father. The two were more alike than either cared to admit—strong willed, sometimes to the point of stubbornness.

"I thought I would go in with Dixon," Vaughn began. "That way we wouldn't have to expose either—"

Sydney shook her head emphatically. "No. I'm going. After Korea, I may have already been exposed. There's no sense in anyone else taking that risk."

"I was in Korea too, Syd," Vaughn reminded her.

"I know the building and the security codes. I'm going." The tone of finality in Sydney's voice told Vaughn this was an argument he couldn't win. He hadn't expected to, even though he felt compelled to try.

Vaughn looked at Dixon. "You okay with this?" he asked. Dixon was, after all, the team leader.

"It's Syd's call on this one," Dixon answered. "This kind of risk . . ." He shrugged. "Her call."

"Then it's settled." Sydney shoved up her sleeve and held her arm out.

Vaughn gave her a crooked grin, and she saw a twinkle in his eye. "Marshall was very specific. This shot doesn't go in your arm."

Sydney and Dixon, with Vaughn as backup, were in place before the sun set. In the daylight, a nearby construction site teemed with activity and the nondescript van didn't attract any attention.

As the site grew dark, the construction crew left for the night, moving off in small groups. Soon, the site was deserted.

Inside the van, the three agents sat silently, waiting. As soon as it was dark, Sydney and Dixon climbed out.

"Merlin," Vaughn said over the comm, "Outrigger and Phoenix are in play."

"Roger, Shotgun," Marshall replied. "Lights out as soon as I have their signal.

This time, knowing the security measures, Dixon and Sydney were able to infiltrate the building very quickly.

"Phoenix," Marshall said when Sydney attached the override monitor to the loading dock switch, "you are not going to believe this."

"What is it, Merlin?"

"The security codes? The ones from last night?"

"Yes?" As Sydney watched, the lights on the monitor flashed red, then immediately turned green.

"They haven't changed. Can you believe that? They install a top-level security system and don't even cycle the codes?"

Sydney was already at the door, entering the warehouse. "Hard to believe," she agreed. "But I'll take it."

They moved quickly through the building, once again encountering no one.

When they reached the balcony, Sydney

opened the small door to reveal the card reader and numeric keypad. She attached the decoder and started the sequence.

Dixon took up his position on the opposite side of the door, his weapon drawn and ready.

The three digits from the previous night were stored in the decoder memory. The display on the keypad confirmed that the digits had not been changed. The counter flickered and another digit displayed. When the last digit flickered and held, the glowing warning disappeared and the door unlocked with a loud click.

The door swung inward and air seeped into the room beyond, as though pulled by a steady vacuum. Sydney and Dixon exchanged a glance and a nod.

"Shotgun, this is Phoenix. We have the door open and we're moving in."

Sydney knew her father, Marshall, and Sloane were listening in Los Angeles, and Nadia and Weiss were online at the safe house. But she addressed Vaughn, since he was her immediate backup.

It was reassuring to know she had a connection to her friends and family. She was part of a network, a team, whose members supported and sustained one another.

Beyond the door was a man without those connections. She pushed the thought from her mind and concentrated on what other dangers might be hidden behind the partition.

It was time to find out.

She pointed to the door, and Dixon acknowledged with a thumbs-up.

Weapons raised, they went through the door nearly together, only a fraction of a second separating their entrances. Sydney moved right, and Dixon left.

The room was small and empty.

The outer door closed behind them. They were trapped.

Two strong fans whirred in the ceiling as air was pumped into the room. Syd sniffed but could smell only the faint ozone-tinged scent of refrigerated air.

They waited, not knowing what might be in the air being pumped into the room. But after a few seconds, the fans cut off and a door slid open on the opposite wall.

The room was an airlock, designed to prevent the atmosphere in the room beyond from leaking out.

Through the open doorway, Sydney saw a large,

brightly lit laboratory. It was like an expanded, well-equipped version of the lab she had seen in Korea. Marble countertops, covered with test tubes, beakers, and expensive testing equipment, lined two walls. The third wall was made of tempered glass, with offices beyond, like on the production floor below.

The fourth wall was a giant white board, covered with equations, formulas, notes, and scribbles. All of them were in Peotr Alexyeev's cramped, precise hand.

They had found Alexyeev's lab.

A crash drew Sydney's attention, and she whirled to the left. A tall, gaunt man in a white lab coat stood next to the countertop, a plastic beaker on the floor in front of him, its contents draining onto the tile.

They had found Alexyeev.

The scientist backed away from Sydney, his hands held out in front of him, as though pushing her away.

"Stay away!" he shouted in Russian. "Don't come near me."

He ran for the glass-walled offices, but Sydney cut him off. She walked toward him, and he ran the other way, trying to reach the door.

Dixon blocked his escape. He was trapped between the two agents, with no other exits.

"Dr. Alexyeev?" Sydney's voice was low and gentle. She took one tentative step toward him.

"Dr. Alexyeev?" She repeated the question, though she knew it was him. It was the man in the photographs from the bunker.

"No. Nonononono." The words were one long, moaning sound, torn from Alexyeev's throat.

"We're here to help you," Sydney said.

"You can't help." Despair was thick in Alexyeev's voice, and he continued to back away from Sydney. "No one can. Just stay away. Don't make me hurt you."

"You can't hurt me," Sydney replied, taking another step. "Nothing you can do will hurt me."

"Yes, I can," Alexyeev insisted.

He was backed against the counter now. He slid along it, working his way toward the door, but Dixon moved into position, forcing him to stop.

Sydney was only a few feet from the scientist. Alexyeev shrank away, his back bowing against the counter, trying to stay as far from Sydney as possible.

"I can kill you. I don't want to, but I won't be able to stop it. Just go away."

Alexyeev covered his face with his gloved hands, as though trying to shield Sydney from his very breath.

"Peotr." Sydney used his given name deliberately. The man was terrified, badly disturbed. She hoped it would calm him.

"You can't hurt me, Peotr. I've had the antiviral. I am resistant, just like your wife—like Ming."

Alexyeev's eyes had widened at the use of his first name. His hands had relaxed a fraction. But the mention of Ming sent him into fresh hysteria.

"I killed her. Her and Uri and the girls. And Kai Kono. So many deaths. Everyone I touch. They all die."

"You didn't kill Ming," Sydney said.

"Yes. Yes, I did." Alexyeev took his hands away from his face and stared into Sydney's eyes. "I killed her with my lies. If I had told her the truth, if I had accepted the responsibility, she would be alive. All I wanted was to create an antidote, something that would protect my children, but I failed. I couldn't save them, and I couldn't save Ming."

Alexyeev's eyes burned into Sydney's, the depth of his grief and self-loathing evident in his expression. "He made me kill Kai. Bound me to a hospital bed and brought her to me, made me infect her. I couldn't speak, couldn't stop her from touching my hand."

The nightmare played itself out in Alexyeev's memory, the horror of that moment clearly reflected on his face.

"Now I am here, a captive. He doesn't allow me glass, for fear I will harm myself. But I won't—not until I know he has been stopped."

"And we're here to help you," Dixon said. He moved closer to Alexyeev. "We know you tried to stop him once before, Doctor. You went to the police in Vladivostok."

"Peotr," Sydney said, "we understand. Really, we do. We can help you stop Jing, and we can help you rebuild your life. When we're through here, we can take you back to the United States with us. There are places where you can continue your work."

"I can't go anywhere," Alexyeev replied. "I am a carrier. Sometimes, when I was in remission, I could go out in public. I could move around a city without worrying about who I might infect. But I can't do that anymore. The disease has changed. There are no more periods of remission. I am contagious all the time."

"We'll get you medical help," Sydney said. "We have scientists who can work with you."

She could hear herself pleading for Alexyeev's help, and for his life. She wanted, needed, to end his isolation.

Alexyeev was surprised at the amount of knowledge these two strangers possessed. The woman said she had been to his lab in Korea, a lab he had thought was well hidden. The man knew about the aborted attempt to turn himself in. The woman knew about Ming. Was it possible they could really help him?

Alexyeev looked at Dixon. "Tell me how you can help."

There was a spark of hope in Alexyeev's voice. Sydney vowed to make sure that hope was fulfilled.

"It's really simple," Dixon said. "We give Jing what he wants."

While Dixon and Sydney briefed Alexyeev, Vaughn, Weiss, and Nadia put their own part of the plan into motion.

Once Alexyeev accepted Dixon and Sydney's help, he provided information about the facility and Jing's organization.

"That door you came through locks on its own," he said. "I am a prisoner in here, and now you are too."

Sydney held up a finger. "Just give me a minute," she said. She left Dixon and Alexyeev talking quietly and examined the door.

As Alexyeev had said, it was locked from the outside.

"Merlin, can you unlock this?"

"I think so, Phoenix. I'll have to establish a link to the decoder and cycle the door. The codes are already stored, so it should be easy once I have the link."

"Let me know when you have it," she replied.

"Merlin should be able to get us out of here," she said when she rejoined Dixon and Alexyeev. "Just take a few minutes."

"I can't leave," Alexyeev said. "Jing will expect me to be here. If not, he won't show. Jing is cautious—paranoid, really. He has many enemies, the ones that are still alive. He is a man who inspires fear, and he buys allegiance, but there are very few people who are loyal to him, and he knows it."

"But how will he know if you are here? He can't see through the walls, can he?" Sydney felt a sudden adrenaline rush. What if Jing had sensors in the lab? Did he already know they were there?

"He'll send one of his lieutenants. Unless the man—it will be one of the two or three that he trusts—reports back that all is well, Jing will not come. I have to be here."

"How thoroughly will he check?"

Alexyeev looked around. "If you mean is there anywhere in the lab you can hide, the answer is no. They check everywhere and scan for surveillance devices. Like I said, he's paranoid. Not that he doesn't have reason to be." He gestured at the two agents. "You two are proof of that."

CHAPTER 25

Inside the warehouse, on the production floor, Sydney and Vaughn waited. Dressed in tactical cold suits to hide their body heat from Jing's infrared scanners, they huddled under a piece of machinery, hidden by the musty tarp.

Dixon, Weiss, and Nadia were stationed around the perimeter, ready to move in.

In the lab, Alexyeev had made the call to Jing. He had told the relay operator he had something, and Jing should come at once.

Sydney listened to Alexyeev's conversation over

the comm link. They had left a device with Alexyeev, which he would destroy as soon as Jing's men entered the building.

Once the device was destroyed, Alexyeev would be on his own until the APO team sprung their trap.

"Tell him I have a solution to our transmission problem," Alexyeev said. It was the one thing guaranteed to get Jing's undivided attention. "I have what he's been looking for."

Within minutes, a black sedan drew up in front of the warehouse. From a vantage point across the road, Dixon watched two of Jing's guards unlock the front door and enter the warehouse.

"They're inside," he reported.

A burst of static confirmed the destruction of the device in the lab. Alexyeev was now cut off from the team.

Sydney forced herself to remain where she was. She worried about Alexyeev. What if he somehow gave away the plan? What if Jing slipped through their fingers again, as he had in Yemen?

She had to trust the rest of her team. If something went wrong, they were here and they would back her up. She wouldn't let Jing get away again, wouldn't allow him to ruin any more lives.

"They're back out," Dixon reported. "Getting in the car."

From his observation post, Dixon watched the men through powerful field glasses. "One of them is making a call," he said. "I'm going to see if I can pick up anything."

He drew a parabolic microphone from his pack and aimed it at the car window. Although the window was closed, he was able to pick up pieces of the conversation.

"Phoenix, Shotgun, this is Outrigger. They are calling for the boss. They say there is something he has to see. Looks like this is it."

Sydney tensed. They didn't know how long it would take for Jing to arrive. All they could do now was wait.

Sydney and Vaughn sat in the dark. Syd wished she could talk to Vaughn, but anything they said would be heard by the entire team.

In the dark, Vaughn reached out and took her hand. He squeezed her fingers gently, his touch a reassuring connection in the silence. She returned the pressure and smiled to herself. There would be time to talk later. For now, it was enough to know that Michael was there with her.

They sat like that for about twenty minutes, until Dixon's voice came over the comm link. "Shotgun, Phoenix, this is Outrigger. Our guest has arrived."

"Let's hope it's the real one this time," Sydney said. Somehow, though, she knew it would be. Alexyeev's bait was too tempting for Jing to send another ringer.

"He's got three men with him," Dixon reported. "They're carrying automatic weapons. There's a driver, too, but he's staying with the car. They're through the door, Phoenix, and headed your way. Good luck."

From their hiding place, Sydney and Vaughn could hear voices in the reception area.

They waited for someone to come into the production area, but no one did. It was clear they didn't know their security had been breached.

Sydney and Vaughn waited until the voices died away. The men would be at the top of the stairs, maybe even in the lab, with no way out.

They had them.

The two agents moved swiftly and silently, passing down the short hallway and into the deserted lobby. They climbed the stairs and approached the lab door. Sydney quickly attached the decoder and entered the password. The door swung open as before and they ducked inside.

When the inside door opened, Sydney and Vaughn had their weapons drawn and ready. But Alexyeev was alone.

"He heard you coming," Alexyeev said. "An alarm of some sort on the door, one I'd never heard before."

"Where is he?" Sydney shouted. The alarm wasn't the issue, Jing was. She had to catch him before he escaped again.

Alexyeev pointed at the giant white board. One end was pulled away from the wall. "There was a door behind there," he said. "I didn't know it existed."

Vaughn didn't hesitate but ran for the board, ducking behind it. Sydney was on his heels.

The door had a digital lock. Marshall had told them Jing didn't change his codes, and Sydney hoped he was right. She entered the code from the front door.

The door swung open, revealing a staircase. Sydney ran down the stairs, Vaughn at her heels. Above them, she heard the door slam shut, and they were plunged into darkness.

Sydney didn't slow down. She ran the rest of the way in the dark, feeling for the bottom of the stairs. As she ran, she dug in her pack for a flashlight.

At the bottom of the stairs was a simple security door with a crash bar. She plowed into the door, emerging at the front of the building.

A few feet away, scrambling into the waiting car, were Jing and his three guards. The driver had kept the engine running. Two of the guards shielded Jing, pushing him into the backseat of the waiting car. As soon as he was clear of the door, the driver shot away.

Behind her, Vaughn shouted. Sydney ducked as he fired his Sig Sauer at the fishtailing car. The rear window shattered, spraying glass across Syd and the guards, but the car didn't stop.

The guards scattered. One of them, a swarthy man with a dark goatee, headed directly for Sydney.

Vaughn continued firing at the car. A rear tire exploded, sending the vehicle into a spin. The driver fought for control.

Sydney caught the goateed guard in the midsection with a back kick. Pivoting the other direction, she landed a chop along the side of his neck, knocking him to the ground.

The car came to a stop. It was pointed directly at Vaughn. The driver gunned the engine, though the flat tire prevented him from getting up to speed. Vaughn stood his ground, firing at the oncoming vehicle. At the last minute, he dove out of the way. The windshield exploded as his last shot found its mark.

The car lunged past him. He fired again, this time hitting the driver's door, and scrambled to his feet. He saw Dixon running across the street, his weapon drawn.

Two of the guards had Sydney, who struggled in their grasp. The goateed man, doubled over at the pain in his stomach, was flailing at her.

Vaughn raised his weapon, but he couldn't get a clear shot. Dixon sped toward him. "Stay on the car," he shouted.

Vaughn turned back in time to see Nadia and Weiss running after the car as it careened across the construction site.

The back door burst open and Jing tried to jump, but he caught his foot in the dangling seat belt. The car raced ahead, out of control. Weiss and Nadia tried to reach it, but it was moving too fast.

Dixon rushed past Vaughn. Two guards still

held Sydney while the third tried to hit the struggling woman.

Dixon ran straight at the goateed man. He tackled him low, dragging him down, and slammed his head against the asphalt of the parking lot.

Sydney, freed of her goateed assailant, turned her attention to the two men who held her. She relaxed against one of them, gaining a tiny bit of leverage. With a rush of movement, she drove her elbow deep into the man's throat. She felt resistance, then a crunch, as the blow crushed his larynx. The man released her, his hands grabbing for his neck.

As the car continued its wild ride, Jing was dragged along, unable to extricate himself. The construction site was uneven, pockmarked with holes and littered with debris, and the car bounced and jolted uncontrollably.

As Vaughn watched with mounting horror, Weiss suddenly grabbed Nadia and threw her to the ground. He covered her with his body.

The car sped on, racing directly toward a parked earthmover.

It never slowed.

Jing was still hanging from the door when the car slammed into the earthmover and burst into flames.

Dixon sprang back up, rushing the last guard. He caught him in a chokehold, forcing him to his knees.

Vaughn looked around. Sydney was running for the front of the warehouse.

"Sydney!"

"I'm going for Alexyeev," she shouted back before disappearing through the front door.

Syd rushed up the stairs and quickly keyed the combination into the keypad. She jittered impatiently as she waited for the air lock to cycle.

When the door opened, Alexyeev was waiting, fear and hope flashing across his face. When he saw who it was, hope won.

"Did you catch him?" he asked. The desperate tone of his voice was like a knife piercing her heart.

"Yes."

"Then it's done? You stopped him?"

Sydney thought of the mangled heap of metal in the construction site. "We stopped him—for good, this time."

Alexyeev breathed a sigh of relief. A sob escaped his lips, and he leaned against the countertop.

"It's over," he said. "Finally, it's really over."

"Yes. It's over." Sydney held out her hand. "Time to go."

Alexyeev pushed away from the countertop and stood straight. His eyes were clear, and the look he gave Sydney was determined.

"I'm not going."

"You have to, Peotr. We have a place for you. You'll be safe, and you can continue your work. Maybe you can finally find a cure."

She remembered the makeshift lab in Korea. "You'll have everything you need."

"Except my family."

Sydney shook her head. "We can't change that, Peotr. We all lose people, but we have to keep trying."

"I don't." He looked around the lab. "This place, this work, it's a danger to everyone. As long as the work continues, there's the chance the virus will escape."

He placed one hand on his chest. "As long as I continue, there's the danger of an epidemic. I can't live with that possibility any longer."

Sydney stood her ground. "We can guarantee your safety."

"At what cost?" Alexyeev cried. "I can continue

to work, as long as I never touch another human being? As long as I remain locked away, where no one sees me? Where no one can reach me? To only leave my lab in that suit?"

He turned his back on Sydney, his shoulders heaving with the intensity of his emotions. "Do you know what it's like to be trapped, alone? The weeks in that suit were torture. I can't live like that."

He turned back, his face once again calm. "I decided, when Ming"—he swallowed hard—"when Ming killed herself, that I didn't want to live anymore. I had nothing to live for. But Colonel Jing found me. I tried to get away, to stop him, but you know what happened. And he punished me by making me a murderer—again—by making me kill Kai Kono."

Sydney nodded. She understood Alexyeev. His disease was a threat to others, but it was a sentence of a living death for him. A life of isolation, a life without human contact, was no life at all.

What Arvin Sloane wanted didn't matter. This was Alexyeev's life and his decision.

She could stop him. He was frail, and she could simply overpower him and force him to go with her. But she couldn't force the man to continue in the living hell that was his life.

Sydney backed away as Alexyeev picked up a beaker from the countertop.

"You're sure?" she asked. "You have my word, we will do everything we can. . . ."

"Thank you, but no. I am sure. You better leave now. This lab, all the experiments and notes, will all be gone soon, and me with it."

Impulsively, Sydney stepped forward. Alexyeev pulled back, but she laid a hand on his arm. "I have the antiviral, remember?"

She leaned in and brushed her lips against Alexyeev's cheek. Her eyes were wet, and she turned away before he could see her tears.

Sydney retreated to the door behind the white board and keyed the security code. The door cycled open.

She stood in the open doorway and looked back. Alexyeev raised one hand in a wave. "Thank you."

"Thank you," she replied. "You helped us stop Jing."

Alexyeev didn't reply. He reached for a flask of chemicals on the bench and slowly poured the contents into the beaker on the counter.

In the beaker, a chemical reaction created clouds of smoke that boiled over the sides and ran along the countertop. The smoke rolled over the edge of the counter and began to crawl across the floor.

"Go!" Alexyeev said. He took a matchbox from its place on the counter. He lit one match, producing a tiny flame.

Holding the flame, Alexyeev picked up a bottle and drank deeply.

The sedative took effect almost instantly, and Alexyeev dropped to the floor. For a split second, Sydney was tempted to run back and drag him out of the lab.

Then the spark hit the smoke, and flames filled the room. The heat drove Sydney back, and the door slammed shut, trapping her in the emergency stairwell.

As she ran down the stairs, she could hear a chain of explosions coming from the lab above her.

She burst through the door, nearly knocking Vaughn to the ground. He grabbed her, hugging her to him.

"We heard an explosion—"

"Alexyeev blew up the lab," she said. "I couldn't stop him. He had it all planned. I barely made it out."

Dixon, Nadia, and Weiss crowded around in time to hear the end of her little speech.

Nadia reached out and drew her sister into a brief embrace. "I am glad you did," she said, her voice husky.

"Me, too," Sydney said. "Now let's go home."

CHAPTER 26

Sydney glanced around the conference table as the debriefing concluded. She hadn't actually lied about the scene in the lab; she'd just omitted some details.

Fortunately, Sloane's relief at their safe return had overridden his disappointment at losing Alexyeev.

She kept her expression carefully neutral as Sloane concluded the meeting.

"Losing Peotr Alexyeev was a great disappointment," he said. "We had hoped to be able to gain a great deal of knowledge from him."

The thought of that knowledge in the hands of

Arvin Sloane terrified Sydney. She felt a surge of relief, knowing he wouldn't have the opportunity.

"However," Sloane continued, "we did stop Gai Dong Jing, and we have effectively destroyed his organization. For that, we have all of you to thank, but especially Sydney and Dixon. Sydney in particular took enormous risks to apprehend Jing."

Sydney smiled a little. The praise meant nothing, coming from Sloane, but she was pleased the mission had been a success. And she was relieved that Sloane had believed her version of the events in the lab.

"You did a good job, people. You have a great deal to be proud of. Thank you all."

The debriefing broke up, and the team trickled out of the conference room. Around the office, the team members made small talk as they gathered their coats and briefcases, getting ready to go home.

Nadia and Weiss stood close together, talking in low voices. Weiss waved Marshall over.

Sydney saw Marshall nod, and Weiss grinned.

The three agents moved apart. Weiss walked toward Dixon and Vaughn, who stood near Vaughn's desk.

Nadia approached her sister and hooked one arm through Sydney's. "Eric is taking me out for pizza," she said. "How about joining us?"

"No, I, uh, I don't want to intrude," Sydney said. "It's your date."

Nadia laughed. "It's not a date, Sydney. It's just pizza. He's asking Dixon and Vaughn, too."

"I don't know," Sydney said. "I'm kind of tired. Maybe I'll just go home and take a hot bath."

Nadia withdrew her arm. "Okay." She shrugged. "Buy you know you're welcome." Nadia walked a couple of steps, then turned back. "Sure you won't change your mind?"

Sydney shook her head and turned away. A bath sounded like a good idea. She would enjoy some quiet time, alone.

Alone. Like Peotr Alexyeev had been alone. She knew what that was like. It was how she'd grown up—only child, dead mother, distant father. For years it was the only life she had known.

But unlike Alexyeev, she had a choice. She didn't have to be alone. She had proven that again and again. She had her friends and her family. She even had a sister.

Sydney grabbed her purse and slung it over her shoulder.

"Hey," she shouted at the group walking down the hall. "Wait for me!"

Christina F. York has written for the Star Trek publishing program, alone and in collaboration with her husband, J. Steven York. The author of Alias: *Strategic Reserve*, she lives in Lincoln City, Oregon.